GUNSMOKE JUSTICE

It had been a long ride—all the way from the Bitterroot mountains of Montana. Brad Jordan was a big man, leathery and saddle-tough, but he was tired now and feeling mean, knowing the girl was waiting for his answer . . . *knowing it meant killing* . . .

'Water and land for everybody,' he mused. He put out a hand as if to feel the dirt. 'It's a good country,' He looked down at the girl and made his decision. 'It's worth fighting for.'

GUNSMOKE JUSTICE

Louis Trimble

GUNSMOKE

First published in the UK by Corgi Books

This hardback edition 2008
by BBC Audiobooks Ltd
by arrangement with
Golden West Literary Agency

ISBN 978 1 405 68216 9

British Library Cataloguing in Publication Data available.

Printed and bound in Great Britain by
CPI Antony Rowe, Chippenham, Wiltshire

GUNSMOKE JUSTICE

Cast of Characters

BRAD JORDAN had come all the way from Montana to find this place. He didn't intend to be scared out.

OLAF HEGSTROM was as quiet as he was big. But when the killing began, he was there.

TIM TEEHAN wondered what one man could do against a crew of hired gunmen.

IKE QUARLES ran the Double Q spread and hired the killers. He intended to own the valley.

JIM PARKER went up against Quarles first. He was smashed.

NEWT CRADDON had been whipped once. But he was Quarles' man—he would try again—from ambush.

ANGUS McFEE was the law in Sawhorse Falls.

FAITH McFEE was his daughter. She wondered if the law was always legal.

JUNE GRANT owned the Split S. She wanted to make a fight of it.

DAVE ARDEN was foreman of the Split S. He made some night rides.

CHAPTER ONE

THE RAILROAD Brad Jordan had been following angled southwest at Spokane Falls. He left it there and headed northwest into the desert of central Washington Territory. In three days he came to the place where the Sawhorse River quit the timbered hills for the sand and sagebrush. He stopped his horses at the fork in the wagon road. One branch went due north, through Knothole Gap into the Sawhorse Valley, while the other wound on across the desert into the coulee country.

He hoped that this time he would reach the end of the road. So many times in the past years it had seemed so, but always there had been something to turn him aside, to lure him on into the next valley or over the next range of mountains. He hesitated now, fearing another disappointment. But in his gray eyes was the stubborn perseverance of a man who refused to be denied, and he reined the palomino and his pack horse north and headed into the gap.

As he climbed the trail, the rocky bed of the Sawhorse dropped farther and farther below on his left. Looking down now and then he could see the stony bed with only a trickle of water running down the middle. It was surprising in view of the heavily treed watershed of the mountains to the east and north; more so since he had heard that this country was well-watered at all seasons of the year. But in this early summer season the river appeared ready to dry up. It might mean nothing, or it could mean a lot. But the thought that nature might have gone wrong gave him a feeling of disquiet.

Too many things had gone wrong for Brad Jordan.

He wondered if the end of this ride would be the same as all the others. The hot, dusty trail, the search for land where a man might settle and create a solid, sure life for himself, the emptiness that came with the bitter realization that men were the same everywhere and that the coming of settlers meant restrictions that galled a free man's soul.

Brad's hands clenched on the reins, pushing their edges into the tight flesh of his fingers. It had been over a year now since the last time he had tried to settle down. And almost that long since the desire to find something better over the next range had drawn him on again. Always following such a period, there was the time of disappointment, of working for another stake, of taking up another search.

Across the Bitterroot Mountains in Montana he had heard of the Sawhorse Valley. A few words casually dropped by a man beside him at a saloon bar had brought questions from Brad. The answers, as always, seemed to be those he sought. A new country, fine grass, moisture, a land where a man could put down roots and grow, creating while he lived.

Brad had waited to hear no more; nothing was changed. The old pattern repeated itself once more. The news of a new place, the long ride, the hope surging up in him until he had to curb his mounting impatience.

He rolled a cigarette now, letting the horses take a leisurely pace. He was a tall man, well-built, but with the bleak look of a rootless drifter. He knew that it was coming fast to him, the pointless life of a man without his own land, no matter how he fought against it. Up to now only the saving humor that came when he was caught in a tight fix had helped him. Many more times of finding his hopes smashed and the humor would be gone, too. He wondered what men did when they reached the end of desire and there was nothing but another trail stretching ahead.

At the summit of the gap a brawling stream no thicker than his arm tumbled out of a crack in the rocks above to spill into a natural basin. Beside this basin a long, low log building had been set to catch travelers tired after the steep uphill pull going both ways.

Brad put his horses at the tie rail along with a half dozen others and a team and buckboard. One bay gelding, he noticed, was drooping with weariness and good for little besides fishbait. The horse had been well cared for, but from the look of it, its owner must have faced hopeless odds in keeping it alive any time these past two years.

Leaving his horses to cool before watering them, Brad walked out of the hot sun into the coolness of the log building. It was a typical freight stop, holding a barroom to his left and a small place to eat on the right. He could smell the stale cooking of too many meals fried in rancid grease and the stale sweat of too many riders working the long days away from home camp.

At the saloon door he stooped, taking in the scene in front of him with the quiet look of one who had walked into many situations of the same sort. Five men, cowhands by their clothes, had a sixth ringed in the center of the small floor. They were cutting into the monotony of the long day by hoorawing the other. For a moment Brad could not understand this, as the single man was a good head taller than any of the others and half again as wide. His hat lay on the floor near his feet encased in heavy work shoes, and his yellow hair was plastered to his skull with sweat.

He showed no fear even though—as Brad saw now—

he wore no gun, while the five men ringing him did. His face was round and open and on it there was still a piece of a smile, as though he was not quite sure of the joke. Hands like great red hams hung down at his sides, the palms open, and his shoulders were rigid and straight in the discipline of a military man. His clothing was nondescript, none of it of a kind usually seen in cattle country.

So far the men had not seen Brad. And the leader, a squat, barrel-shaped cowhand, waved his gun. Amusement flickered over his whiskered face. "Sing us some Swede, you!" He laughed aloud. "Do us a Swede dance."

Brad had seen it too many times, and each time the disgust rose in him. Sometimes it was a Chinaman, sometimes a Mexican who had drifted across the border, occasionally an Irishman too weary from laying rails to fight. This time they had got a Swede, which would be a special kind of fun since it was more of a rare thing.

The big man swiveled his head, looking from one to another of his tormenters. Slowly the last of his smile went away as he realized there was no joke to this at all. He spoke in slow, careful English, making each word distinct.

"What you do this for? What I do to you, hey?"

"Sing us some Swede!" the bulky cowhand said again. He thumbed back the hammer of his gun and sent a shot through the big man's hat near his feet.

Brad put his hand over the bone handle of his .44. This was not his fight, but then many another he had mixed in had not been his, either. The man on the short end of the odds appealed to him. He had never stopped to figure deeper into his reasons.

As the sound of the shot faded into the acrid smell of gunsmoke, footsteps hurried from the rear of the building and Brad whirled to see a girl burst out of a door near him. He had a glimpse of red hair, dark as his own, piled under a ridiculous riding hat, a long riding skirt below a man's flannel shirt, and a lightly freckled face that was pretty even when flaming with anger.

"You stand there!" she said scathingly.

Brad said, out of his surprise, "No, ma'am," and took a step into the room.

The men inside looked up now, and the one with the gun out of his holster scowled. "This place ain't open for business," he said. "Ride on, you."

"It's open for my business," Brad said quietly. He took a quick sideways step, getting in behind a lanky cowboy before the man could move out of the way. With this momentary protection, he drew his own gun. "Now," he observed, "it's sort of even."

The lean man in front of him moved his arm and Brad got him by the wrist, throwing the arm up against the man's back until he held still. The one with the gun stood very still; he was held back now unless he wanted to shoot through his own partner to get at Brad. No one else moved.

"Just toss your guns on the other side of the bar," Brad said.

"Damned if I will!" the barrel-shaped man answered.

Brad gave the arm he held a twist upward. The lanky cowhand howled and reached his left arm around to his gun. When he had it drawn, he threw it awkwardly. It hit the bar top and clattered to the far side out of sight. Brad pushed a little more, without gentleness.

"Get about it, Newt," the man groaned. "He's busting me."

The big man in the center looked around with a puzzled expression. "Back out, mister," Brad ordered, "and get their guns."

Newt shifted as the big man made a move. From the doorway the girl said, "Hold it, there!"

Brad threw her a quick look, enough to see that she held a rifle casually in her arms. But there was nothing casual about the look on her face. Newt seemed to sense it, too, for his gun went behind the bar to join the other. He stood sullenly, the hatred on his face a livid thing.

The other guns followed as the big man got behind the rest. Then Brad let loose of the lanky cowhand and holstered his own gun. A glint of sardonic humor touched his gray eyes. He unbuckled his gun belt and handed it to the girl in the doorway.

"I like things even," he said. He looked at the big man. "They weren't fooling, friend. You make something of it now, or they'll run you ragged from here on."

The big fellow seemed to have difficulty in catching the words. But finally he nodded. "Fight? Yah!"

"Yah," Brad agreed, and the pleasure of battle touched the high planes of his face and lingered at the corners of his mouth. "I'd say it was about even if the lady won't interfere. How about you, Newt?"

The barrel-shaped man wiped his hands on his jeans. "This ain't your game."

"I chose to make it so," Brad answered shortly. "All right, friend, let 'em see what the weather's like outside."

The big man said, "So," in agreement and reached out one huge hand. The five men bunched, not yet ready to call it off. Brad laughed softly and waded in. Five to two, but the big one was worth a dozen.

Brad saw his hands take two men by the shoulders and bring their heads together with a cracking sound that rang through the room. The lanky cowhand threw a fist and Brad side-stepped it, landing a blow that brought blood spurting from the man's nose. Brad laughed again and drove his left into the man's middle, sending him hurtling into Newt. Angrily, Newt threw the man back and jumped forward. Brad caught him with a shoulder, driving him against the bar and holding him there with a hip.

He said, "I don't like your kind of fun." And chopped both hands at Newt's face. He chopped again, and when a glaze came into Newt's eyes he stepped back. Newt made a wobbly forward move, and Brad straightened him with both hands, cutting viciously with all the pent-up hatred he felt for the kind of thing Newt had been doing. Newt turned and folded over the bar, hung there an instant, and then slid soggily to the floor.

Brad jumped around, but there was no need. The big blond man had two by the shirt collars and was dragging them from the room. He went out past the girl, sweating no more than he had been before, and there was a thud as the men landed on the dirt outside. He came back and helped Brad with the others. A broad smile crossed his round, sunburned face.

"Good fight."

Brad nodded, and went to the girl for his gun belt. She handed it to him without a word. "You own this place?" he asked as he buckled on the belt.

"No. Tim Teehan does."

"And where might Tim Teehan be right now?"

"Waiting it out," she said. There was no scorn in her voice for Tim Teehan. "Those were Double Q men."

"It means nothing to me," Brad said. "Tell Teehan we'd like a beer to wash the taste of this out."

Tim Teehan appeared then, coming to the bar from

someplace in back. He was a small, wizened Irishman, and there was no love for himself written on his face. "On the house," he said.

Brad glanced outside. The lanky cowboy had staggered up and was pouring water from the basin onto the others. Laughing, Brad went to the bar for his beer. The big man joined him, smiling widely now.

Brad looked at the girl who still stood in the doorway. "Is Double Q so bad?"

"You're going into the valley?" she countered. She was a tall girl, standing straight with the rifle butt down at rest now. She showed little pleasure in what Brad had done.

"I intend to," he told her.

"Then stay in town," she said flatly. "Double Q won't bother you there."

"I don't figure on Double Q bothering me anywhere," Brad said, and tipped up his beer. Beside him the big man drained his glass with a great sigh of satisfaction.

The girl was still watching Brad. "You enjoyed that fight," she said.

He studied her, noticing for the first time that her eyes were the same gray color as his own, and that there was a strength in her face he seldom saw in a woman. But when he spoke he was puzzled. "You wanted it," he pointed. He nodded in answer to her statement. "A fight sometimes takes the edge off a man." He felt better; too long on the trail had sharpened him too fine. A little honing always made him feel better. It was that way with most men, he knew. He saw nothing strange in it.

"You cut Newt Craddon up deliberately," she accused.

"I don't like his games," Brad answered. The point of this was beyond his interest. He had joined the fight in passing, now he was done with it. He pushed out his glass for another beer. The important thing still lay ahead and he wanted to get to it.

Tim Teehan started the beer across the bar toward Brad when his eyes focused on the doorway. "Look out!" he cried, and dropped behind the counter.

Brad swung and saw Newt in the doorway, a rifle coming up level in his hands. Brad took three steps from the bar to the girl, shouldering her to one side as the gun blasted. He caught her as she lost balance and swung away, reaching for his own gun.

The bullet went into the bar where Brad had been standing, and the rifle cracked again as he made a snap shot. Newt disappeared, leaving smoke and the ringing echo from his gun. Brad saw where his bullet had chipped wood from the doorcasing and he ran that way.

The men outside were on their horses and spread. Two rifles fired, driving Brad back to cover, and then the thud of hoofs beat the air and the riders were gone.

Brad came back, holstering his gun and looking toward the girl. She stood white-faced, her lips tight. "They'll wait for you on the road now."

"I'll need my other beer, then," Brad said, and moved into the saloon.

The big man was standing with his back to the bar, staring down a little stupidly at his own left hand. Blood ran from his fingertips to the floor, and a red stain was spreading across his dust-plastered shirt high on the shoulder.

He looked at Brad in wonderment. "Shot," he said, and his voice was full of pained surprise.

CHAPTER TWO

His name, Brad discovered, was Olaf Hegstrom. The pain from the rifle bullet that had gone through his shoulder caused the sweat to pour down his face, but he made no sound at all.

With the girl's help Brad made a crude bandage out of the available supplies at the Knothole Gap rest stop, and on her advice he decided to take to the hills, rather than follow the wagon road down into Sawhorse Valley.

At first he hadn't believed her, but a short trip to a point of rock where he could look down on the road showed him that she was right. Newt had split his Double Q crew into two groups, and they had the road blocked just below the summit and out of sight in both directions. Brad returned tight-lipped to the building.

"I'm going in," he told her.

She measured him with her cool gray eyes. "You're the kind who would," she said. "Even if you weren't heading that way."

"You don't like me, do you?"

"I don't like brutality," she replied.

"Sometimes there's only one way to do things," Brad said. His humor came, twisting his lips sardonically. "My way." When she made no answer, he went on, "How about this Olaf Hegstrom, you said his name was?"

"Yes." She looked toward where Olaf was seated, bandaged now, and staring down, still with the stunned look on his face. "No one knows much about him," she said. "Except that he came nearly a month ago and disappeared into the north end of the valley. Someone said he was building a homestead shack up there. He was in town twice for supplies that I remember.

"Then today," she continued, "I was coming up here and saw him riding ahead. We came up together and he told me he was on his way out to file a homestead. Before we got here I could see the Double Q riders behind us. They came in. And then you did."

Brad rolled a cigarette thoughtfully and glanced at Olaf. "Where is the county seat from here?"

"Three days' ride on a good horse."

"Then," Brad said, "I don't think he'll be filing very soon. I'll take him back to his cabin so he can heal up."

She looked at him strangely now. "You'd do that? They were trying to run him out of here. They've run others out. Now it will be you, too."

Brad smiled at her. "I feel sorta responsible, ma'am. If I hadn't busted in he might have got off with no more than a kick in his self-respect."

"Do you think he's that kind?" she demanded. "To dance for them?"

"No," Brad admitted honestly. "I think he'd have fought and maybe got killed for his trouble. I feel responsible, anyway. Now if you'll tell me how to get around the road, we'll be going."

She gave him brief, explicit directions. Thanking her, he went outside and took the horses to the rear of the building. With a nod to Tim Teehan for the free beer, he led Olaf out. The girl followed, studying Brad's mount and the neat job on his pack horse.

"You've come a long way," she said.

"Drifted," he corrected.

"You're just drifting into Sawhorse, then?"

Brad saw that Olaf was in the saddle, and then he swung up himself. He grinned down at her. "For a pretty girl, you're an awful nosy one."

Color flooded her face and she turned away sharply. He kept on grinning until she was inside the building, and then he pointed to the dim trail rising into the timber and started Olaf ahead.

It was not easy going. The trail was little more than a deer track and as they climbed firs came in to replace the high-branched pines. Some of the firs were spread-branched and these raked Olaf's shoulder cruelly. But he rode without a murmur, seemingly content to trust the man behind him.

The girl had said to keep high and swing to the north near the first ridge. This he did, and when the sun was straight up they reached a shelf of rock that looked down on the valley. Brad pulled up and something inside him hurt a little as he looked on the expanse below.

It was the old feeling, only stronger than it had ever been. He had never seen such a fine layout for a spread. He sat with his hands resting loosely on the saddle horn, his eyes measuring and searching. Down there the Saw-horse Valley lay sprawled out for him to see. It was a long oval, blunted at the north and south ends. The hills on the south through which the gap ran and those on the west about halfway up the valley were mounds of rock and sage. But farther along the timbered slopes of the Sawhorse Range came in, circling the valley from halfway up the west side, around the north and down to the east.

Brad could see the fine silver lines of creeks coming out of the mountains and the gulched bed of the river as it twisted out of the north and flowed the length of the valley, cutting it into two unequal parts. What surprised him were the alternating patches of strong green contrasting sharply with the drab brown of drying bunch grass.

He turned to Olaf Hegstrom. "Looks like irrigated hay," he said.

"Yah, hay," Olaf answered. He lifted his good arm and pointed. "Alfalfa, they call it."

Brad had seen some of it in the valleys of Wyoming. It was pretty much a new thing to him, but he had heard that in this country they winterfed all the stock, due to the heavy snowfalls, and this alfalfa was supposed to give a better yield than native grass.

"They irrigate it?" he asked Olaf.

Olaf moved his arm up and down. "With pump," he said. His broad face creased into a frown. "There's no water now."

It took Brad a little time to get that. He studied the layouts below while Olaf explained. There were only five ranches on the west side, and the two nearest the north end of the valley had water enough to irrigate by horse-drawn pumps. The others were losing their hay. It was interesting, Brad thought as he listened, that the biggest spread, astride the northwest corner of the valley, was the Double Q outfit.

"I've seen that before, too," he muttered, and started off again along the trail.

Olaf turned his horse carefully and then his voice came quietly, swinging Brad around. He spoke his *th* sounds more like a *d* but Brad had no trouble understanding. "They come," Olaf said.

Down below, climbing up on a switchback trail toward them, rode five men. Even at that distance Brad recognized Newt and the lanky cowhand. Even while he watched, one man flung up a rifle and fired. The range was too great for accuracy, but close enough so that Brad heard lead singing through tree branches not ten feet away.

"Can you push that crowbait?" he demanded of Olaf. There was a nod, and he said, "Let's ride, friend!"

The trail was plainer here on the ridge and for a while Brad felt they were gaining. It was a flat bench with a steep slope down and a line of rimrock breaking into the sharper edge of the high mountains above. There was no getting off of it here, and he pushed the horses to the limits he thought they could stand.

They were perhaps halfway along the valley when he glanced back and saw the first man outlined on a rise. He said, "They're closing in."

Olaf Hegstrom turned a pain-lined face toward Brad. "You go down," he said and pointed toward the valley. Brad saw a narrow trail cutting its way steeply down the slope. It was something he could make. It was not a trail Olaf could handle, wounded as he was and riding a jaded pony.

"Keep going," he said briefly. He looked back again and there were two riders in sight. Then the trees swallowed them momentarily. Brad leaned over and loosened his carbine in the saddle boot.

"Those jokers mean business," he muttered, and wondered if their pride held so deeply that they would take this time to chase him and Olaf.

When two more bullets clipped branches not far above them he knew that whatever it was, they did mean business. He saw that Olaf was slowing, and now the trail rose again, ascending sharply and then flattening out on a ledge that gave no cover for a good half mile.

"Start climbing," Brad ordered. "And stay low in the saddle." He swung his rifle free.

Olaf looked at him and at the gun. "I stay," he announced doggedly.

Brad gave him a grin of understanding that brought light through the dullness of pain in Olaf's blue eyes. "You're in the way here," he said. "Take my pack horse. I'll catch up."

Olaf was silent a moment as if weighing it. "Yah," he said, finally. And when the pack horse was tied to his rig, he started up the precipitous slope.

Brad slid off his palomino and led it out of sight behind a screen of timber and buckbrush. Then he moved beside a thick-boled cedar where he could get a view of the trail. He held his fire though he saw a man appear some distance away. Turning once, he caught a glimpse of Olaf and the horses plodding along the open ledge now—fair game for anyone who got this close.

Brad lined his sights and waited. There were two trees not a hundred yards ahead forming a natural frame for anything that rode between them. The first man was the lanky cowboy, and he carried a rifle in shooting position. Brad shifted his own gun a fraction and fired.

The horse on the trail neighed shrilly and reared up. The rider's howl was loud in the silence of the forest as the bullet caught his shoulder, driving him back and out of the saddle.

There was a boiling noise from behind and Newt came in sight, firing and riding low as he put his horse around the downed man. Brad levered and waited until Newt's shot had clipped bark from above him. He shot, but Newt's twisting run caused him to miss. Then another man appeared, and Brad sent a hurried shot that he knew was too low. The rider's horse jerked as a foreleg shattered, and the man went crashing over its head and lay still.

Now there was only Newt. And he seemed crazed with the desire to get to Brad. A shot whined into his hat, jerking it from his head and he answered, still riding a twisted trail to make himself a poor target.

Then he was close enough and Brad dropped the rifle and palmed his .44. He sent three quick shots, none of which made its mark, but the hail of lead slowed the man in front. Momentarily, he hesitated and then swung into the brush. Brad listened to the crashing until he decided it was receding, and then he waited a while longer.

At last two riders appeared, coming cautiously. One put a bullet through the head of the downed horse. The other captured the riderless one and they hoisted the lanky cowhand and the other aboard and led them off again.

"Through for now," Brad said to himself, and holstered his gun.

Olaf was far ahead and, mounting, Brad put the rifle back in the boot and spurred up the trail after him. When he was on the flat, narrow trail of the ledge there were a few futile puffs from far below and sprays of rock blossomed behind and above him. But they were going, not coming, and the angle and distance were bad for good shooting. Brad rode on without concern.

He caught Olaf at the end of the ledge where the trail dipped into the timber, and they rode on more easily. It was nearing early dusk when the trail, having kinked northward, took a downward pitch.

While there was still enough light to see, they came to a crude log cabin, sod-roofed and set in a grove of firs. There were holes for two windows and a third hole for the door. But inside Brad found it clean with a packed earth floor and a bunk built into one corner. A sheet-iron stove sat under an open canopy chimney made of clay and wattles. There was practically no equipment except for a few pans and a coffeepot.

"This is it," Brad said. He helped Olaf down and inside onto the bunk. It creaked under his massive weight as he lay back with a sigh of weariness.

"Barn," he said and pointed.

"I'll find it," Brad told him.

He located the barn, a lean-to built on the rear of the small cabin. Inside there was a sack of grain, and near the door a small stream had been caught in a wooden V trough. Brad tied the horses inside, unsaddling them and taking the pack off the third. He carried it to the cabin and dropped it on the floor. Olaf Hegstrom—as if in Brad lay safety—had fallen asleep.

Brad worked while the light lasted. When the horses were cooled, he gave them water and a little grain and then staked them at the edge of a natural grassed bowl that sloped southward. He estimated it at close to forty acres, and wondered if Olaf had intended to farm this land.

The horses taken care of, he found an ax and cut a supply of poles and some fir boughs. It was dark inside the cabin now and he located a lantern and lighted it. Then he made a pole bunk in one corner as Olaf had done.

Olaf awakened as he was building a fire. He pushed himself to a sitting position. His shy smile reached out and touched Brad. "Thanks, friend." There was a question in his voice.

"For now," Brad said.

Olaf studied the answer carefully. "For now. For later," he said. "You go. I go."

Brad remembered the sight of the valley. "Maybe," he said, "I won't be going. Not if I find what I want here," he added.

When he was ready for sleep he set his rifle handily beside him. This was the familiar pattern repeating itself; he knew it too well to lose caution. The Double Q riders weren't through. Their vengeance might be temporary, but it was fire-hot right now and they wouldn't rest until it was taken.

CHAPTER THREE

"A QUEER ONE," Tim Teehan said, as Brad disappeared into the hills. He looked at the girl, who was preparing to leave. "The kind we need, you think, Faith?"

Faith McFee said doubtfully, "Wouldn't it be replacing one kind of bully with another, Tim?"

"You think him a bully?" he asked. He wiped at his bar with a soggy cloth. "And he thinks me a coward." His wizened Irish face wrinkled distastefully. "And maybe I am. But what can one man do against a hired crew?" He shook his head slowly. "I'm getting old, Faith, and like your uncle says, peace is worth a lot."

There was no scorn in her for him. She understood both this man and her uncle. They had done their share of living and now they wanted to sit in the shade and rest. Not many years were left for either man. His wide mouth quirked in a gentle smile.

"You're an odd one," Tim Teehan went on in a slow voice. He drew himself a beer and sipped at it. "Angry at Dave Arden for holding off against Quarles' Double Q, and angry at this man who dared to fight them."

"Not angry," she said. "Frightened maybe, Tim. There was something cruel in the way he went after Newt Craddon."

"Ruthless, maybe, but not cruel," Tim amended. "Newt is the kind you reason with by using a club. Hold your judgment," he advised her.

"I always try to," she answered, and started for the door. "Tell Molly I'll be back. And I hope she's better soon."

"Molly has a strong heart," Tim said. "And remember that. A man wants a woman with a strong heart in this country."

18

"I'll try," she said again, and went out to her buckboard.

It was not a long trip to the town of Sawhorse Falls. The wagon road looped a short distance down the side of the gap and then followed a gentle grade to the floor of the valley. From there it was not a half hour with a good team to the edge of the town. Faith hurried her team once it was safe to do so. The trouble at Tim's had taken more time than she had planned to allow herself, and it would be almost time to open the restaurant for supper when she got back.

She drove automatically, the buckboard now empty of the presents she had taken up to Tim's sick wife. Her mind was on the man she had met, and she frowned a little because he kept recurring to her. There had been something appealing about him and, at the same time, something frightening. Studying it, she decided that Tim's word had been the right one. There was a quiet ruthlessness about the stranger. And yet she had felt his humor. Womanlike, she sought for a weakness in the man, and felt a vague desire to save him. From what, she was not quite sure. But in the man there was strength. And to see it misdirected in a brutal battle bothered her.

As she reached the valley floor, she forced her mind to the land around her and the problems of the people with whom she was most concerned. The ranches to the east were not yet bothered by the Double Q's driving expansion, and so she gave them little thought. But those two places on the west slope, from this end of the valley as far up as Nick Biddle's, were her friends. And it was about them she felt the most concern.

The southernmost ranch was Jim Parker's "experiment" as men had first called it. They had laughed and gibed when he came packing a bag of books and sacks of seed. But when he showed them how to get hay without depending on the native grass for winterfeed, their laughter stopped and turned to interest.

And, from the time of Jim Parker's coming, there had been trouble. Until then Nick Biddle and Ike Quarles had seemed satisfied to do as the rest, running what stock they could feed through the winter. But this business of irrigating hay gave Quarles, a shrewd man, the chance to grow big—and so he was taking it. The legality of his way was questionable, but what was legality where there was no law?

Once more Faith McFee thought of her uncle. He was the law in Sawhorse Falls but, for the same reason that Tim Teehan refused to fight, he refused to be the law beyond the town limits. Cowardice? She had never thought of Angus McFee as a coward. He had faced down more than one would-be gunman in his town and had won without needing to shoot. But how much of a true test had he ever taken?

She pushed the idea away. These were disturbing thoughts, ones she would rather not face. There was still the chore of daily living to do and it was this she had now to concern herself with. Someday, perhaps, the valley would have the peace it had once known. Until then what could she do, or Tim Teehan do, or any one man do?

Again she remembered the quick hardness of the stranger who had come in and challenged the Double Q crew. "One man," she murmured aloud.

Perhaps, but one could stand against twenty for just so long.

Faith had the supper nearly prepared and was opening the door of her small restaurant when the noise of a group of riders boiled up from the street. She stepped to the board sidewalk and shielded her eyes against the slanting rays of the late westering sun. They were coming in from the north, and she recognized Newt Craddon in the lead.

She watched tensely as he went by, riding solid in the saddle, a deep scowl of anger on his bearded face. Behind him came the other men, with the last leading a horse on which two men rode. One, the lanky cowhand she knew as Clip, rocked with the pain of a bleeding shoulder.

Her uncle stepped from the door of the jailhouse next door, and now both watched until the riders reached the far end of the street and went around the side of the One-Shot Saloon.

"Going to Doc Stebbins," Angus McFee said to Faith. He was a small man, weathered and sharp-faced with the air of a plucked bantam about him. "They didn't stop to check their guns."

"They hardly had time," she pointed out, "with a wounded man to take care of."

"No guns allowed in town," he said sharply. "They know it."

"There are times——" Faith began.

"There ain't no time," he snapped at her. "If that law ain't kept, there'd be fighting every time a Double Q man rode into town." Pulling at his gun belt, he walked briskly down the street toward the One-Shot.

Faith sighed. He was right in his way, of course. By enforcing his ruling of making every man check his gun, the sheriff had kept the town peaceful. Because he had been here and had been the recognized law from the time Sawhorse Falls was little more than a single trading post, the law was old enough to be accepted without question. Men checked their guns automatically, picking them up when they left town. What fighting was done was without bullets until men stepped beyond the imaginary lines McFee had drawn around the town.

Faith waited until he was out of sight. Then the clerk from the general mercantile, a short way up the street, came in for his meal and she went back inside.

"Excitement," he remarked. "Looked like a Double Q man got shot." He sounded a little surprised, as if unable to think of anyone who would dare draw against a Double Q rider.

"Seems so," she said, and brought his coffee.

He was about finished when the dealer from the Sawhorse Saloon directly across the dusty street came in for his supper. Shortly after, the blacksmith's boy, Jube, put his head in the door. His freckled face shone with pleasure at so much going on.

"Double Q boxed some stranger on the high bench east," he panted. He was the carrier of news, and he never failed to bring it first to Faith.

"Who says so?" the dealer wanted to know.

"One of Coe's riders in town," Jube explained importantly. "Him and Coe saw some of it. The stranger was holding Newt and his crew off, and that big Swede was riding the ledge trail going north. Then they saw the stranger going up. He had a big palomino. And Newt and his men coming back with Clip shot up and Baldy knocked cold!"

He pulled his head back abruptly and ran off to spread the story elsewhere. Faith, dishing a plate for the dealer, felt a muscle-shaking wave of relief. When Jube had first begun to talk she pictured the drifter and Olaf Hegstrom caught on the ledge by the Double Q crew. Such a trap would have been easy enough to fall into for a man inexperienced in the country.

But, after a moment, the relief went away and her mind formed another picture—a picture of the tall, lean man with eyes the same color as hers, standing off Newt, smiling as he shot Clip from the saddle, and she wondered what in a man's past would give him pleasure in cruelty.

The restaurant started to fill, buzzing with the excitement of an accident to Double Q, and Faith was too busy to do more than work. Jube's sister Colly came panting in, late as usual, and donned an apron to help. After that it was easier, but even so there was work enough to keep her mind from what had happened.

The last of the regular diners were gone when her uncle came in and sat down. She fixed a plate for him and one for herself, waiting for him to give her the news.

"I had a little trouble," he said. "Newt was riled." He sucked at his coffee and bobbed his head. "But I got their guns."

"What about Clip?"

He looked up, taking a moment to remember Clip. "Shattered an arm. Reckon he'll live."

She felt an impatience at this concern for nothing but his own primary interest. She said, "Did they say what happened?"

"Didn't ask," Angus McFee answered.

No, she thought, he wouldn't. The valley was no concern of his. She called, "Colly, will you bring more coffee?" and settled down to eating.

Newt Craddon sent Clip and Baldy home in a hired rig and walked by the alley behind the westside stores to the rear of the Sawhorse Saloon. Here, at the back, was a door opening to a flight of steps. At the top was a hall, and at the front end of it was a room he entered after knocking and being told to come in.

The owner of the Sawhorse Saloon, a tall man, thin

to emaciation, was sitting behind a desk. He motioned Newt to a seat on the sofa.

"The boss come in?" Newt demanded.

"Too early," the tall man said. "Biddle was here. He rode out before you came."

Newt's disregard for Biddle was contemptuous. "I'm going hunting, Keinlan. You tell Quarles some joker got the jump on us. He sided with the Swede."

Keinlan nodded as if it was little concern of his. "I'll tell him."

Newt got up restlessly, the scowl deepening on his face. "The Swede headed for home, I figure." At the door he turned. "And tell Quarles that Parker's at the One-Shot in a poker game."

Keinlan's long face twisted. "I thought Quarles told Parker to stay out of Sawhorse." The twitch came again; he was laughing. "Double Q's having a little trouble making its orders stick."

Newt swore at him and went out, slamming the door. Keinlan leaned back, rubbing his fingers thoughtfully over his lantern jaw. There was a good deal in this to interest him. When a man like Quarles was faced with trouble, it could be worthwhile to see how he fought it. He had been waiting for Quarles' first weakness to show up. Carefully, he planned the way in which he would pass Newt's information on to Quarles.

CHAPTER FOUR

BRAD WAS A MAN who had developed infinite patience in the past years, and now he found it necessary to call strongly on it against this eagerness to seek out land to settle on.

He felt a more immediate duty to Olaf Hegstrom, and so he stayed by the big man during the first dangerous week of his convalescence. There were a number of things Brad found of interest on the homestead. Olaf had come too late in the season to do much in the way of farming, but he had planted a garden in a clearing behind the house and now Brad, with as much help as Olaf could give him, built a rail fence around it to keep out the ever-present deer. It was no easy chore and more than once Brad wondered at the tenacity of home-steaders.

This business of swinging an ax in cutting and trimming endless poles was something he could not fathom. The idea of breaking good ground for a crop when all a man had to do was to put beef stock on the grass was something else beyond his understanding.

Olaf, in his slow-speaking fashion, made it plain that he could not comprehend a man who did not care to raise the food for his table out of the good earth. When he and Brad were at the garden, he would bend between the rows to pull a weed or cover the partially exposed roots of a plant. And sometimes when he stood up he would hold out a handful of rich dirt for Brad's inspection. There was the love of the soil in his every movement.

And yet, despite the fundamental differences, Brad knew that he and Olaf were basically the same. A strong bond sprang up between them, based not on Olaf's gratitude or Brad's feeling of responsibility but on mutual respect.

Olaf, Brad learned in the long days, had been a sailor until a few months ago. From the age of ten, when he ran away to sea, he had known only ships. But after fifteen years of sailing, even though he had risen to mate, his desire drove him back to the land.

"I heard of homestead land," he told Brad. "In Seattle I leave my ship and come across the mountains." His broad smile came with the memory. "Green," he said. "Green and fine in the springtime. But they say, 'That is government land for cattle in the bottom.' So I come up here; the land is better. There is more water." He paused, and added wistfully, "My father had a farm like this."

"You're not bothering any cattlemen up here," Brad said. "Why'd they try to run you out?"

Olaf's only answer was a puzzled shrug. He did not know. "In town at the saloon once," he said. "But they had no guns." He flexed his huge right hand. "I fought and they left me alone. But up there in the gap it was different."

Up there, Brad agreed, the Double Q had meant business. But he could not understand why any ranch would bother a homesteader who had taken forty acres of grass and a hundred and twenty acres of timber, not all of it level. The place was not even adjoining any ranchers' land.

They finished the deer fence before dinner. No one had bothered them in the past week. It was as if there were no one within a thousand miles aware of their presence. This in itself was suspicious to Brad. He had known too many of Newt's kind not to wonder why the Double Q had not swept down on Olaf before this. Town, he thought, might be a good place to find a few answers and find information about land.

Restlessness was eating into his patience, and now that Olaf had the use of both hands he felt he could take the time to make a trip.

He put the last poles on the deer fence, thus finishing a structure higher than a deer could jump and with the poles too close together for one to climb through.

Outside the main fence and a foot away was a single-pole fence three feet high. Deer, he pointed out to Olaf, frequently jumped straight up, and with this extra fence there would be no way for them to do so.

"There," Brad said, "the farm's all yours. I want no part of it."

Olaf was sucking on a foul-smelling pipe and he removed it from his mouth, regarding Brad gravely. "No land?"

"Lots of land," Brad said. He looked down at the rolling forty acres of grass in front of Olaf's shack. "A man's no good foot-loose, Olaf. He needs his own dirt with a house on it to keep out the weather. And maybe a woman inside." It was back on him, this hunger for things he had never had.

"But," he added with a faint grin, "I'll take mine in beef."

Olaf knocked his pipe out into loose dirt, stepped on the ashes and stood up. "We go to town now," he said slowly. "You've stayed away long enough."

"Mind reader," Brad said, and went to saddle the horses.

When they were ready, he dragged his spare gun from his war bag and handed it to Olaf. The big man took it without question, thrusting it into the waistband of his jeans. Then, mounting carefully, he led the way down a gentle trail to the valley floor.

They went through graze dotted with cattle wearing a half dozen brands. This was bunch grass country, and the beef looked contented enough and fat enough so they did not seem interested in the fenced hayfields on the valley slopes. The road began a half mile after they left the last hill and the going was quick after that.

The valley interested Brad as it might any man looking for a place to light. There was always that dream of a spread—a spread like the one he had always craved. And this was fine country to dream on.

Towns interested him, too. Towns, he figured, had the character of the men who built them and the men who controlled them. As he and Olaf drew closer, he could see that this town was like a hundred others in the west. The wide, dusty street with false-fronted buildings stretching a block or two, a few houses scattered here and there, nothing more. Sawhorse Falls would have a few saloons, a blacksmith shop, a general store. Maybe a jail and a hotel with a dining room. It wouldn't look like much. It wouldn't mean much to a man until he got to know the people.

Brad drew rein suddenly as a sign loomed up on his right. He stared at it in astonishment. It was neatly lettered and explicit enough.

It read, "TOWN LIMITS OF SAWHORSE FALLS. NO FIRE-ARMS ALLOWED. LEAVE ALL GUNS AT SHERIFF'S OFFICE. THIS MEANS EVERYBODY."

"I'm not going into any town without my gun," Brad said. Certainly no town where this Double Q might be. Not when he knew that men like Newt were still around.

He started forward again. The river had slid over toward the road here, and on his right he could see the skeletal remains of the mill that must have given the town its name. A quarter of a mile inside the town limits they came to the first buildings. A livery barn was on the east, and just below it a solid-looking general mercantile. Most of the houses seemed to be east of the main street, though there were a few shacks set back between the buildings fronting on the west and the river.

Down from the mercantile was a small restaurant,

and next to it a log structure that Brad recognized as a jail. Across from these were the Sawhorse Saloon and a decrepit structure labeled Sawhorse Hotel. Some distance down from the hotel was the One-Shot Saloon.

Toward this saloon Olaf led the way. "Better beer," he told Brad.

"I'll go along," Brad said. He looked around curiously. It was midafternoon now but there was no one on the street. The restaurant was closed, and there was not even a single horse tied along the street. It was almost too quiet.

"A saloon's a handy place," he remarked as they tied in front of the One-Shot. "On a hot day it quenches a man's thirst. On a cold day it warms him. And," he added softly, "if there's information, the saloon's where you'll find it."

"Yah," Olaf agreed. "Good beer."

Brad led the way into the building. His face was devoid of expression, though he felt an urgency pushing at him now that he was in Sawhorse Falls. He pushed aside the batwing doors and strode into the cool dimness of the saloon. It was not large and it was nearly empty. A single poker game was going on near the rear, and two men were drinking at a table across the small dance floor from the bar. The bar itself was empty except for the bartender, a dark-faced man with a drooping mustache and a doleful expression. His eyes opened wide when Brad and Olaf came up to the bar.

There was a slight pause in the conversation of the two men across the floor, and momentarily the clink of chips ceased; then, as Brad looked around, both began again with more fervor than before.

"Beer," Brad said to the bartender.

The man brought it. "Say," he said, "ain't you the

one that——" He broke off suddenly as the doors swung open. Backing off, he reached under the bar and put his hand on a lead-weighted bung starter.

Brad turned. A man nearly as tall and wide as Olaf Hegstrom had come in. But, where Olaf was solid, this man had a loose flabbiness about him that hinted at soft living and indulgence. His belly pushed against his shirt, trying to overflow his belt, and his jowls hung with weight, quivering slightly as he walked. He moved with surprising grace as he stepped toward the bar.

Now the conversation and the rattle of chips ceased entirely. The two men across the dance floor stood up and backed against the wall. One made his way with soft, sliding motions toward the rear.

The newcomer caught sight of Brad and Olaf, and he paused in full stride. His eyes, set deep in his heavy face, were almost obscured by pouches of fat, but Brad could see the shrewdness in them. He stood a long moment and then his head jerked.

"So you're the drifter."

Brad had been braced before, by drunks and by men who had heard of him and were anxious to use him for a notch on their guns. But this man was neither drunk nor full of desire to kill. There was something coldly ominous in his deep voice, and hardness that Brad could feel lay underneath the flabby exterior. Years of drifting, searching for one thing, had taught Brad to measure men. In this one he saw, besides the shrewdness, an iron will.

The bartender slipped up behind Brad, and his words were barely loud enough to be heard. "That's Quarles. Double Q."

Brad's smile was easy, touching his stubborn mouth but not reaching his gray eyes. "I'm the drifter," he said quietly.

Quarles took the rest of the step he had started, nodded abruptly, and came on up to the bar. He ordered a whisky and deliberately turned his back to Brad and Olaf. He had not come for this, Brad thought. His concentration was on something else; his manner obviously relegated the problem of Brad to the future. And so Brad waited to see what had brought him to a saloon where he was clearly not wanted.

It came quickly. One of the poker players, a short man with broad shoulders and the slim hips and stomach of an athlete, left the table by which he had been standing and moved to the end of the bar. He put an elbow on it, hooking one booted foot over the brass rail so that he faced Quarles. His face was lean and smooth-shaven, with a dark beard struggling up through the skin.

"Whisky, Abe," he said to the bartender.

When Abe finished serving, he moved to the bottle rack, leaning on it nervously, one hand still clutching the bung starter. He was wishing the Doc had this shift right now. He might be a poor hand at owning a saloon, but he was a good one when it came to stopping trouble. Failing that, he could be counted on to patch up the remains after a fight. But, like every afternoon, the Doc would be asleep in his office. Abe shifted his grip, getting a firmer hold on the bung starter.

Quarles was the first to speak. "So you came to town anyway, Parker."

"It's Friday," Parker said in an unruffled tone. "I come to town every Tuesday and Friday."

"I told you last week to get out and stay out."

Now the saloon was completely silent. Not a man there wanted to put himself on record as favoring Jim Parker over Ike Quarles but in the stillness was an evident sympathy. One poker player chose that moment to shift his chair aside, and the grating sound it made was hideous in the stillness.

Parker sipped at his whisky. His cool voice was tinged with insolence. "I'm going into pigs this fall, Quarles. You open to a proposition?"

Abe let out a slow, audible breath. Quarles' voice ignored the insult. "I threw you out last week. This time they'll carry you out."

Brad could feel the temper in the man and he wondered at his judgment that here was an iron will. Quarles was trembling; there seemed to be something about Parker that cut into his reason.

Parker finished the whisky and set down the glass. "That was last week, Quarles," he said, and took a step toward the dance floor.

The invitation was too plain to miss. Abe had the bung starter ready, but Quarles was amazingly quick. He stepped out of reach before Abe could get into position. Swiftly Quarles came up against Parker, one hand going for Parker's shirt front and getting a grip. He threw his weight contemptuously, sending Parker spinning across the floor to crash into a table on the far side. The smaller man got slowly to his feet, one hand pressed to his ribs. His face was a blank mask.

Quarles went after him, his heavy legs driving like train pistons. His arms were up, waiting like twin pile drivers. His eyes were almost lost in the fat of his face, but what could be seen of them turned every watcher in the room cold inside. No man had dared bother Ike Quarles before.

Parker waited silently, balancing on his toes. When Quarles came within reach, he flicked out a hand and stepped lightly aside. His knuckles raked Quarles' fleshy nose, drawing blood. Quarles bellowed and stepped in, his arms flailing. Parker struck again, moved again. Now he had his back to the room and plenty of space in which to work. Quarles turned like a gored rhinoceros.

Quarles' face began to show the blows. One eye was cut, the other puffing. His lips were flattened against his teeth, and his cheekbones looked as if they had been raked with red paint. He panted as he kept going in on Parker, his breath coming heavily through his heaving chest. He looked done, beaten, but the cunning stayed in his eyes and the steadiness of his movements never wavered.

Parker feinted once too often, got one step too close. His fist licked out and struck. And then Quarles had a grip on his arm and was drawing him close. Parker lashed with his other hand, but the blow scarcely ruffled Quarles' hair. He lifted the smaller man, grunting his effort, and crashed him to the floor. The boards creaked and Jim Parker could only lie and shake his head.

Quarles bent and jerked Parker to his feet. He held him at arm's length and drove his fist viciously forward. The blow made a soggy sound against Parker's cheek. He reeled back, off balance, and crashed into a poker table, carrying it over and scattering chips and glasses across the floor. He held onto the table with his hands, using it as a prop while his head cleared.

Quarles bored in again, implacably. Parker sucked deep breaths and waited for him. When Quarles reached, Parker straightened suddenly and lashed out with the last of his strength. As soon as his fist struck he knew it was a mistake. He could feel the smashed bones in his right hand.

Quarles stepped back, hesitated a second, and then fell on his face like a great tree toppling. He rolled and got to his knees and hung there, his massive head swaying. Dust from his fall swirled around him and through the dust came his hoarse, bull voice:

"You had your chance, Parker. Now you'll go in a box."

Slowly he rose, one hand gripping a splintered club made of a chair rung. Parker was standing, his hands dangling helplessly, the strength gone from his body.

CHAPTER FIVE

B RAD HAD WATCHED the fight with interest. For all Parker's lack of size, he had been in a fair fight. Brad was no man to interfere when all things were open and equal, but when Quarles went for Parker with the piece of chair rung, Brad figured there was an end to waiting. Fairness had gone. Quarles' plain intent was to beat Parker's brains out.

Brad reached for his gun. His voice was quiet but it carried even to the anger-dulled ears of Quarles across the room. "Beat him with your fists or quit," he said flatly.

Quarles swung his head, showing glazed eyes that took a moment to focus on the gun. It scarcely seemed to register, and he turned back toward Parker. "Go to the devil," he said thickly, and took a step forward.

Brad knew he could never make it across the room before the club swung down. He did the next best thing. His shot was harsh in the close confines of the saloon.

Ike Quarles bellowed in amazement, staring at his empty, numbed hand. Once more he swung toward Brad. "Just who in hell are you, drifter?"

Brad's dry humor that always came when he felt the closing in of tension appeared now. His grin was idle and a trifle insolent. "Referee," he said cheerfully. His eyes flickered from Quarles to the other men, but no one seemed at all interested in doing anything. He holstered his gun. "Looks to me like——" He broke off as Jim Parker took a plowing step forward and fell to the floor. He lay still, with wisps of dust settling around him.

"Looks like it's over," Brad amended. He touched the butt of his gun. "Now don't get the idea of stomping anybody."

Quarles stared at him a long, still moment. Then he went to where his hat lay, picked it up and put it on his head. He walked slowly toward the door.

"This town ain't for you," he said softly.

Olaf had moved near the doorway. His left hand hung stiffly, but his right was up, cocked. "I let him out?" he asked.

"The place needs airing," Brad said. "Let him out."

Olaf went to the bar; Quarles stepped through to the street and the doors settled slowly after his passing. A sigh like the rustling of aspen leaves went through the room and the poker players came forward to look after Jim Parker.

"Beer," Olaf said hopefully.

"Two," Brad said. He knew he had taken the wrong step again. The devilish amusement that came to him when things got tight had got him in more than one set-to. Quarles, perhaps, could see the equality in not being allowed to brain a defenseless man, but he would never forget being ridiculed and forced to walk out without making his stand.

Abe brought the beer. His eyes were bulging and they looked very curious right now. "You never see a gun?" Brad asked.

"Not in this town."

"With things like Quarles crawling around, you need a gun or two," Brad told him.

"Who's doing this shooting?" a shrill voice demanded

suddenly. Brad tasted his beer, sighing in pleasure at the coolness, and looked around at the owner of the voice.

He saw a small, dried-up man with a weathered face and a squared-off, strutting air about him. Brad's eyes dropped to the star on the man's shirt front and then down to the pearl-handled gun on his hip. There was anger on his sharp face.

"I was," Brad said. He felt the humor working up inside him at the obvious annoyance of this sheriff.

"You're under arrest! No gun toting allowed in the town limits."

Olaf stirred, setting down his glass. "He bother you, Brad?"

Brad cut him off with a quick movement of his hand. It was Abe who spoke up. "He was only stopping a killing, sheriff. I'm glad he had the gun."

McFee pushed out his lower lip. "Reasons don't matter," he said firmly. "When a man comes into this town, he checks his gun. That's the law."

It could have been funny, Brad thought, only the sheriff was plainly in earnest. He said, "That's a new law to me."

"There's signs at both ends of town." The sheriff thrust forth his head, his blue eyes bright and hard.

"To tell the truth," Brad drawled deliberately, "I smelled beer so strong I didn't stop to do any reading. Now, if you want to check this gun——"

The sheriff put out a skinny hand. Brad marveled at the simplicity of the man. It would be easy to throw down on him and walk out free. But there was an air of confidence about McFee, as if such a situation would be incomprehensible to him. Obligingly, Brad took out his gun and passed it over. He didn't like doing it, but the sheriff's intensity warned him that he would get little help unless he cooperated. And sometime he might need help badly.

Olaf said again, "He bother you, Brad?"

Brad looked at Olaf's gun. "Give him yours, Olaf," he said. The sheriff snatched it ungraciously.

"Now start hiking!" he ordered.

"Wait a minute, McFee," Abe protested. "This ain't no regular case. This man's a stranger and——" He broke off, swallowing back his words under the sheriff's withering glance.

King around here, Brad thought and, still grinning, he let the sheriff march him and Olaf out to the street and into the small jail building. As he left the saloon he saw three men carrying Jim Parker somewhere to the rear. Once more he had mixed into another man's business, Brad thought, and once more he had got into trouble for it. Yet he knew he would do it again when the time came. It was too deeply ingrained in him to expect a change.

"Our horses are in that hot sun, sheriff," he said.

"You got money to pay board?"

"I've got money," Brad said, and realized it was a mistake.

"They'll get took care of," McFee said, and herded them both in front of his desk. He took a seat behind it and laid both guns close to his hand. The room was small, with barely enough ceiling room for Olaf to stand upright. Besides the desk, two chairs and a hat rack made from deerhorns completed the furnishings.

With complete seriousness McFee banged a home-made gavel on the desk top. "Prisoners charged with wearing guns in defiance of the law. Prisoners guilty. Thirty dollars or fifteen days in jail."

Brad's jaw slacked. "What's this foolishness?" he demanded sharply. "Thirty dollars!" The humor was leaving him. This was in no way amusing.

The gavel banged again. "One prisoner charged with shooting a gun inside the town limits. Fifty dollars or thirty days."

Brad measured the distance between himself and the guns. But the sheriff's sharp eyes were watching him and he shifted a hand closer to Brad's weapon. "I can't pay that kind of fine," Brad said.

"I know *he* can't," McFee said, jerking his head toward Olaf. He got up and motioned toward the rear door of the room. It opened on a hall that gave onto three cells. Both men were put into cell No. 1, and the door clanged behind them. Brad passed a gold half-eagle between the bars.

"Give our horses better treatment," he said, and turned away.

The cell was small with two iron cots, one on either side of the room, and a barred window, breast height to Brad, across from the door. Brad chose his bunk and sat down to roll a cigarette. Olaf took the other and began to stuff his foul-smelling pipe.

The warm silence of late afternoon descended over everything. Brad tried the view from the window. He could see a little to the north, and while he watched, the sheriff led the two horses across the alley back of the jail and into a barn a short distance away. He came out and disappeared. Brad heard a door slam; he judged it to be behind the restaurant. Otherwise there was nothing to look at. A few scattered houses set in groves of balsam poplars and then sage and sand running toward the eastern mountains, blue with misty haze at this time of day.

He swatted lazily at a fly and turned toward Olaf. He had fallen asleep. Brad went to him and took the pipe out of his mouth, setting it on the floor. Then he crawled into his own cot and shut his eyes.

It was hard for him to realize the sheriff had not been joking. But when he opened his eyes the sight of the bars was all too real. Brad was glad Olaf's farm included no stock; he doubted if the sheriff was concerned about anything beyond the scope of his own short-sighted law.

Brad was brought to his feet by a rattling sound. The door was opening and a loaded tray of food moved into the room. A girl was carrying it. Brad blinked. It was the same girl he had seen that first day in the gap. Olaf awoke at once at the smell of strong coffee.

There was no more pleasure on the girl's full mouth or in her gray eyes than there had been before. She set the tray on Brad's bunk, shut the door, and stood just inside the room, waiting in silence.

Olaf crossed the room and began to eat heartily. Brad looked steadily at the girl. "In trouble again," he remarked to her. He added, "Brad Jordan's the name. It looks like we'll get acquainted this time."

"I'm Faith McFee," she answered. "The sheriff is my uncle."

"Then," Brad told her, "I won't say what I intended." The humor was coming up in him again, stimulated by her obvious disapproval. "Except that now there are two McFees that have no use for me."

"I'm not concerned enough to——" She stopped, and began again hotly, "If you think I approve of this, you're wrong. I heard what you did, and I tried to talk to my uncle."

"Thank you," Brad said sincerely.

A flush crept up her cheeks. "Because of Jim Parker," she said pointedly.

Brad nodded and turned to his food. He was embarrassed by her standing there, but he ate until he was satisfied, rolled a cigarette, and lifted his coffee. He studied her now and wondered at the seriousness in her. A girl that age, not much over twenty-one he judged her, should have a smile on her face and laughter inside. Especially one so pretty.

He said, "What's Quarles got against Parker? Same thing he tried to run Olaf out for?"

"I don't know why he tried to run Olaf out," she said. "But he's afraid of Jim Parker."

"A man that size, with a crew of gunslicks like he has?"

"Some men have more than strength or guns," she said. "He's afraid of Jim Parker's brains."

"He was about to lose those brains," Brad said. "And I didn't see anyone interested enough to help." He was not trying to annoy her. He was looking for information.

Her lips closed tight again. "I know," she said. "I said I was sorry you had to go to jail for it." She unlocked the door and Brad rose, taking the tray to her. She went into the hall, relocked the door, and carried the tray out of sight.

"She's sorry," Brad said dryly. "It's too bad her uncle hasn't half her sense."

Olaf stood up, stretching. "You want out, Brad?" He walked to the window and put his hands on the bars. Brad could see his huge muscles pulling against his shirt, though he was scarcely using his left arm. Bits of dust and splinters of wood stirred where the bars were set into the heavy sill.

Brad said hurriedly, "Not now, Olaf. But it's a good thing to know."

Olaf nodded and went back to his bunk, satisfied. Brad rolled another cigarette and lay back, wondering at the outcome of this. He was a thoughtful, dogged man, despite the carefree exterior he tried to display to the world.

His desires were strong and stubborn, and ever since he could remember, the greatest was for land and a home of his own. His dreams centered around the sight of his own graze fattening his own stock. To him this meant the security he had never known as a boy or man. Land and a house and a woman to share the good things with him.

It was dark outside when footsteps came down the corridor again. McFee appeared, carrying a small oil lamp. He passed it through the bars to Brad.

"What'd you come here for?" he demanded suddenly.

This, Brad decided, was no place to find the answer to his question. "It's a nice country," he said, "A good place for a man to settle."

McFee grunted and strode away. Brad shrugged and lay down again. After a few minutes he could hear voices coming from the office, and one sounded like a woman's. He wondered if Faith McFee were arguing again with her uncle. The voices ceased after a while and the sheriff walked back to the cell door again.

"You want work?"

"I'm a top-hand," Brad said without conceit. "But how does a man with a jail record get hired?"

"Half the men in this valley's been inside here. It took some a while to get used to the law." McFee's voice became clipped. "I'll have none of their shooting. They can keep their wars out of town."

"Ah," Brad said, and the old familiar pattern formed for him again, "range fights?"

The sheriff held out a hand and slowly squeezed the fingers together. "About done now," he said, and let his hand fall open loosely.

Brad said shrewdly, "This Quarles looks like a man who wants everything."

"He wants the valley."

"And the town?"

"He keeps his peace in my town!"

"Like today," Brad said.

McFee glared coldly at him, turned and tramped away. Brad shrugged. "I must have ruffled him up," he said to Olaf.

"You talk good," Olaf said admiringly.

"Not good enough," Brad answered. Rising, he blew out the lamp and returned to the bunk.

The air was beginning to cool off, and outside he could hear the night sounds. Crickets chirped awhile and then retired. A few raucous shouts from the direction of the Sawhorse Saloon rose and ceased abruptly. Somewhere at the edge of Brad's view a house lamp was lighted. Hoof-beats made an insistent sound on the road and then stopped. Before he fell asleep, he could see the first rays of a nearly full moon spreading out over the tops of the mountains.

It was fairly high when he came awake again, the full light of it coming through the window and falling across his cot. At first he thought it was the moon that had wakened him. Then he realized that someone was outside the window. As the person shifted position slightly, moonlight glinted on the barrel of a gun that was thrust through the bars.

CHAPTER SIX

I T WAS THE sound of metal striking metal that awoke him. The man outside was tapping the gun barrel gently against the bars.

"In there. You in there, Jordan."

So his name had got about already, Brad thought. Through McFee, he supposed. He answered cautiously, "Go on talking."

The voice was one that Brad did not recognize. It was thick, as if the owner were trying to disguise it. "I like the way you shoot," the man outside said.

"And what I shoot at?" Brad countered. He lay still, unable to move without attracting attention, and knowing that he was an excellent target from the window. Besides, he wanted to see where the other was taking this talk.

There was a brief, hard laugh. "I come to talk business. You want a job?"

Brad's mind worked swiftly. There was something wrong here. Although he did not remember Jim Parker's voice well, he felt sure this was not Parker. If it had been, he would have given his name, and certainly he wouldn't have to slip up here in the night. On the other hand, a man with the capacity for hatred Ike Quarles had shown was not the kind to turn benevolent and send a man to him with an offer for work. He decided to carry this on awhile longer to see what he could learn.

"I might be," Brad answered.

The man's voice dropped even lower. "There's gunhand wages for a good man. Hundred and found."

This again was the old story to Brad. He had taken a gunhand job once in Colorado. And though he had sympathized with the man who hired him, it had not given him any liking for the work. Killing was a hard thing to stomach, though at times he knew there was no other way. A certain kind of snake understood but one law—a bullet in the brisket.

"I wasn't thinking of that kind of work," he said carefully.

There was a moment's pause. Then: "A man that makes as fine a target as you do right now ain't got much choice, Jordan."

On the other side of the room Olaf had stopped snoring. Brad could hear the soft sounds of his feet touching the floor. Olaf was in complete darkness and, to cover the noises he made, Brad spoke louder.

"That's blunt enough for any man," he admitted. "And it don't leave much choice." His voice stopped as he made out Olaf's bulk beneath the window. He said suddenly, "But if you tried to shoot me, it——"

A surprised howl of pain rose and Brad broke off talking. Olaf made a grunting sound. Moonlight fell on his hand, showing it wrapped around the gunman's wrist. Olaf gave a hard jerk and dragged an arm through the bars until a shoulder stopped it. The gun clattered to the floor of the cell. Outside saddle leather creaked as the man shifted weight in agony.

Brad laughed softly. "Now let's talk business." He got off the cot and came nearer the window. The sill was only breast-high to him and he could see out quite easily. Olaf now had both hands on the man's arm and was applying a steady pressure that threatened to break a bone over the edge of the sill.

Brad had never seen the man before. He had a thin, scoop-shaped face with a dark mustache drooping over narrow lips. Sweat was running down his face and dripping from his angular jawbone despite the chill of the night.

"Maybe," Brad said amusedly, "the sheriff would like to know about this gun toting in his town."

The man swore lividly. Brad was surprised at the reaction he had got. Either the people in this valley paid more respect to McFee's law than he had supposed, or this man just didn't want what he was doing known.

"Tell him to quit, damn it! He's breaking my arm," the man gasped.

"I don't mind if he does," Brad said.

"I'll give you a better deal," the other panted. "Hundred fifty and found, Jordan. You'll be bought out of here and get two months' wages in advance."

"Who're you talking for?" Brad wanted to know.

"That's my business," the man said evasively.

Brad smiled thinly. "Pull harder, Olaf."

There was a low, agonized curse as Olaf applied more pressure. "Parker," he managed to say. "He needs help."

"I know he does," Brad agreed. "Harder, Olaf."

The man's head jerked convulsively and his free hand lifted, then fell back. "Me, damn you! Nick Biddle."

"Ease up, Olaf," Brad said. The man's sigh ran out of him and Olaf relaxed the pressure but kept his grip. "Three hundred dollars won't buy much," Brad told him. He added slyly, "Now I was thinking about getting me a piece of land here. This is fine-looking country. How much land will three hundred buy?"

"I'll give you land. All you want."

"Ah," Brad said, "some of that green hay meadow, maybe? And water to keep it that way?"

The man was silent, his small eyes studying Brad with a new respect. "Water," he said. His laugh was short and harsh. "Yeh, there'll be water aplenty."

"That's the kind of talk I like to hear," Brad remarked. "A man that can promise me water from a dry river." His voice had a silky tone the other could not fail to catch. "Or maybe you make the water some way?"

The man cursed again. "You got your choice, Jordan. Work for me or——"

"Or the land I get is likely to be six feet over my head," Brad interrupted. "I heard that lingo before." He turned from the window and went to the cell door. So far their voices had not been raised, even in anger, but now he lifted his to a ringing shout.

"Sheriff! McFee!"

There was no answer from inside, but a startled Swedish cussword from behind spun him around. Moonlight glinted on a knife blade slashing down. Olaf's grip came loose and the man pulled his hand back through the bars. Brad made the window in two long strides, scooping the gun from the floor as he moved.

Olaf stood to one side, holding one wrist with his fingers. Brad thumbed the hammer on the gun and then let his arm fall. The man had ridden too fast around the corner of the building for him to get any kind of shot at all.

"Danged fool trick," Brad muttered. "I should have known that kind would carry steel. Let's see it, Olaf."

He struck a match and Olaf obediently extended his arm. The wound was superficial, a slashing cut where his right wrist joined the hand. It bled freely, but Brad could see that it was more painful than dangerous.

He handed Olaf a few more matches. "Keep 'em lit," he said, and reached into his pocket. He brought out a bandanna, clean but for a thin layer of dust that had sifted over it. Shaking it thoroughly, he made a tight wrapping on Olaf's wrist. "The bleeding won't last."

Olaf returned the rest of the matches. "He fooled me," he said disgustedly. "What did he want, Brad?"

Brad told him. "And that sheriff is off sleeping somewhere," he added. "I never saw a lawman yet that was where he was needed."

Olaf wriggled his wrist and watched blood slide in slow drops to the floor. "What do we do now?"

"We drift," was the answer. Brad's grin was cold in the darkness. "I've seen his kind before, and you don't set and wait for him twice. He talked this time, but next time he'll shoot first and talk later."

He made a cigarette and lit it. The match glowed against his lean face, bringing out his brooding expression. He said slowly, "I made too good a guess, Olaf.

There's something plenty wrong here. Something to do with water." He nodded, as if agreeing with himself. "It's about time for you to do that strongman trick so we can get out of here."

He went to the window and grasped the bars but, hard-muscled as he was, he could not budge them. Olaf pushed him aside and wrapped both hands around the bars. He gave a deep grunt and twisted, throwing his shoulders into the work.

Flecks of dust and wood splinters rose in the moon-light. There was a tearing sound and the end bar wiggled in its socket. Olaf applied more pressure. Brad could see the pain stretching his mouth tight. Sweat ran down Olaf's forehead and mixed with the blood oozing from his wrist.

"Let it go," Brad said. He was afraid Olaf would do some real damage to his wrist.

Olaf's answer was another grunt and a final, twisting wrench that jerked two bars completely loose at the bottom. After that it was simple. When the bars were free Brad laid them on one of the cots and helped Olaf through the window. He scraped but, by turning his shoulders, he managed it. When he thudded to the ground, Brad hoisted himself up and wriggled through. Olaf's big arms were there to let him down gently.

They stood a minute, listening to the night sounds, and then Brad led the way around the building to the street. He kept in shadow, slipping along quietly, his ears tuned for the sound of a rider coming back.

But it was silent. The street was dark. A faint line of light over the eastern mountains warned him of coming daylight. Nodding to Olaf, he started up the middle of the street, his footfalls muffled by the deep dust.

Olaf spoke. "You want the horses, Brad?"

"I want the sheriff," Brad said. "I've got a little business to settle before we leave town."

"Here," Olaf said, and led the way. They went between the mercantile and the restaurant to reach the alley. Brad saw a fair-sized building attached to the rear of the restaurant. Across from it was the barn where he had watched the sheriff put their horses. "He lives here," Olaf told him.

Brad was glad Olaf was not a man to waste words. Sometimes, it was true, the big sailor used almost too few but, as he told Brad, he had learned his "good English" on a British ship, and so he was easy enough to understand.

Brad took the "here" to mean the house rather than the barn, and he approached the one door. Lifting his fist, he rapped hard on the panel. There was no answer and he rapped again, using the butt of Nick Biddle's gun this time. Somewhere inside, feet hit the floor and a sleepy voice grumbled. Brad kept on rapping, a faint smile on his mouth.

The door was flung open and the sheriff peered out into the darkness. Brad said, "I came to check a gun, sheriff."

"At this time of night?" McFee asked. He sounded half asleep.

"You got a sign says to check my gun," Brad went on. He fought to keep the laughter out of his voice. Obviously, the sheriff hadn't yet recognized him.

"Wait until morning," McFee growled.

"All right," Brad said indifferently. "Where do I sleep? I'm not spending any more time in that cell."

"I don't care where you sleep." McFee started to shut the door when Brad's words made sense. He came awake in a hurry. "Wait! Wait right there." He disappeared for a moment and returned, holding a lighted lamp. He held it higher, letting the light fall on Brad and Olaf.

"Jailbreak! She got you out. I told her——"

"Who?" Brad said, hurriedly. "Whoever *she* is, you've got it wrong. We walked out and no one helped us."

The sheriff's voice was heavy with suspicion. "And then just came here to me?"

"Why," Brad said innocently, "I figured I had to check this gun."

McFee growled and jerked the gun from Brad's hand. "Get on in here," he said. "I don't know what your game is, Jordan, but I aim to find out quick."

Brad and Olaf stepped into the room. It was small but pleasantly furnished. Brad took a chair near the big center table and tried not to laugh at the sight of McFee in a too-short nightshirt.

But when he spoke, the desire to laugh was gone. He told the sheriff what had happened, leaving out nothing. When he was done, McFee's gaze was more thoughtful than he had seen it till now.

"She was right," the sheriff said. "You ain't Quarles' kind."

"What has Quarles to do with it?"

"Nick Biddle is his bootlicker," McFee answered shortly. He turned and put the lamplight on Olaf's crude bandage. Blood still seeped slowly from a tag end of it.

"That might be worse'n you thought," he said. "I'll get Doc Stebbins for it."

"All right," Brad said. "You say this Biddle works for Quarles?"

"No. He thinks he works with Quarles," the sheriff explained. "His spread lays next to Quarles' coming south, between the Double Q and June Grant's Split S. But Quarles has plenty men working for him. You're the first drifter I've heard turn him down."

"Maybe I'm looking for a different thing," Brad said.

"Work, wages, gold—it's all the same."

"No," Brad said. The sheriff was friendlier than he had ever expected to find him. Now Brad tried to explain some of the feelings bottled inside him.

"Land and peace aren't the same," he said. "I want a place where a man can build and keep on building. A man has to have something to tie to." He realized that he was failing in trying to express this to the sheriff, and he fell silent.

McFee seemed to understand, though, at least a part of Brad's feeling. He said slowly, "Build and keep on building. That's what Quarles is doing—but he don't want anybody else to do it. Not here." His shrewd eyes measured Brad thoughtfully. "Maybe that's why your kind fights him. He's got what you want."

Brad could feel the suspicion in the old man's voice. Once more he realized he was up against one of the things that had plagued him for so long. Others could not seem to understand a man's desiring to have something for himself and only for himself. They always thought that once he started growing he wanted to keep on, and get what was theirs, too.

He was close to making an enemy out of McFee, he thought, just as he had in other places with other men.

CHAPTER SEVEN

Nick Biddle rode hard around the corner of the jail using his left arm mostly, because the right was still sore and bruised from handling. He rode without thinking, saving his strength to get free of Jordan and the gun he held.

The horse carried him on across the street and between the Sawhorse Saloon and the dingy hotel, almost to the river. Here he drew up and calmed his breath, listening.

There was no sound of pursuit. Except for a few late frogs croaking, there was little noise at all. He turned the horse and rode back to a small building set behind the saloon. He got to the ground, looped the reins over a handy post, and went to the door at the back of the saloon.

Opening it quietly, he went up a flight of bare stairs to a hall. It was dark, and he cursed as he stumbled over a loose board. Lighting a match with his left hand, he walked on and turned into a door near the front. There was a couch stretched along one wall, and he flopped onto it, laying his bruised arm across his chest.

With daylight he rose, yawning, and retraced his steps to the patient horse. Shivering against the chill of the air, he mounted and rode hard along the river until he was well above town. Then he put the horse to the narrowed road and kept going. The road to his own place branched off shortly, crossing the river at a ford and winding toward the western hills. But this he ignored, keeping straight until the timbered north slopes of the valley were in clear view. Here a road branched west, and he followed it over a bridge, through green fenced fields and up to a squat house on a knoll.

This was Quarles' Double Q. And already a half-dozen hands were stirring out of the bunkhouse, gathered at the horse trough to wash. Biddle ignored them and went up to the front porch and into the parlor. Quarles was there, standing by a stove lighted to take off the morning cold of this country.

"Well?"

"That Swede like to broke my arm," Biddle said.

"And got your gun," Quarles observed, looking at the empty holster. "So you didn't hire Jordan."

"I didn't get him." Biddle was surly and hungry. "Breakfast ready?"

"Coffee." Quarles raised his deep voice, and a Chinese cook stepped into the room. Quarles gave the order and settled closer to the stove. He carefully refrained from saying more until Biddle had the coffee in his hand and a cigarette made.

"Find out anything?" Quarles wanted to know. "What he came for?"

Biddle laughed shortly. "Land. Land and water." He repeated what had been said.

Quarles listened intently, measuring Brad's words, seeking a meaning in them. "She might have brought him in from outside," he said finally.

"And then let him go to jail?"

"To throw us off," Quarles said. He was a suspicious man by nature; he followed the thoughts of others as if they were his own. "Or maybe she didn't tell the sheriff. I hear she was around his office after Jordan got locked up."

"You think, then, she's ready to fight?" Biddle asked.

Quarles' reply was interrupted by the beat of hoofs. He went to a window and peered out. "Here comes Arden now," he said. "He'll know."

The man who came in was lean and young. His face, under a cap of yellow hair, looked innocent until his eyes were noticed. They were small and set close to his thin nose. There were something quick and sly in their blue depths that had more than once held another man back from rashness.

"We were talking about your boss, Dave," Quarles said.

Arden's smile was practiced. "June? She's howling at McFee for putting some cowboy in jail." He laughed out loud, directing it at Quarles. "And just because he took a shot at you yesterday."

"I lost my head," Quarles admitted. "It won't happen again." The stove was glowing red now, and he took a turn away from it. "Biddle here tangled with Jordan and his side-kick, too." He told Arden about it.

Arden listened attentively. He said, "You act spooked about him, Quarles."

"Ike thinks your boss might have brought him in," Biddle explained.

Arden started to shake his head, but stopped. "Could be," he said after a moment. "She don't tell me everything she does."

"She's ready to fight, maybe?" Biddle went on.

Quarles let him ask the questions and contented himself with watching Arden. Biddle he knew well—as well as a man could know another in six years. With him there was nothing to worry about. He was plainly and openly but one thing—a man who wanted all he could get, and who was willing to do what he must to get it. But Quarles knew Arden less completely. In two years their relationship had stayed on a business basis.

That Quarles could understand, since June Grant was not to know that her foreman rode to the Double Q for his instructions. But even so, in two years Quarles felt he should know better what was in Arden's mind. At times Arden gave him the impression that he thought he was bossing Quarles, instead of its being the other way around. Quarles stayed careful with Arden; he needed the foreman. But if Arden should get ideas too big for himself, the need would be less than the danger.

Always Quarles had wanted one thing from life. And

now that it was in sight, at the very tips of his stretching fingers, he was not ready to let anyone move in and stop him. He had not spent his years in this valley to see a fool's greed bury his plans.

All this moved rapidly through his mind as he listened to the talk between Biddle and Arden. Arden said, "She's said nothing to me about fighting. But she's getting restless. She can't afford to lose this year's hay crop. Not with a record drop of calves to feed come winter."

Biddle said meaningly, "Maybe she won't have no stock to feed come winter."

"Let that alone," Arden flared angrily. "If any brand gets slapped on her stuff, it'll be mine, not the Double Q or yours."

"We've talked that out before," Quarles broke in. "It'll keep. It's this Jordan I want to know about."

Arden put out his hands. "I said I don't know." His eyes were small and cold. "But if a man like to broke my arm or shot at me and I thought he was moving in on me, I know what I'd do."

"So you would," Quarles said. "But the town knows he shot at me."

Arden stood up and rolled a cigarette, dropping the flakes of tobacco carelessly on the carpet. "Get a man to give him a poker game or an argument in the saloon. That's one way."

"I'll take care of it," Quarles said heavily. "Now, what'd you come for today?"

"To tell you she was getting restless again," Arden answered.

"You're a fool," Quarles told him. "What if you were seen coming here?"

"I've been known to look for strays before," Arden said without rancor. He smiled a thin smile at Quarles and stepped to the door. "First, I'd see to this Jordan."

He put a hand on the latch. "Don't slow down now, Quarles. Only a sucker goes backward once he's got up full speed."

"I'll handle it," Quarles said. "You take care of your end."

"It needs a month or more for that. Just you be ready when the time comes." Arden opened the door and stepped onto the veranda.

Quarles waited until his horse's steps faded out of earshot. He said testily to Biddle, "He's pushing now. I don't like a man that pushes."

"We need him," Biddle said. "That Parker made more trouble than you figured."

"I'll see to Parker, too." Quarles heard the clang of the bell as the cook put in the call to chow. He started for the dining room, then turned to look back at Biddle.

"Next time you run against Jordan, make sure you finish what you start."

CHAPTER EIGHT

Doc Stebbins was a brusque little man, the general size and shape of a flour barrel. He walked into Sheriff Mc-Fee's house while it was yet too dark to see clearly outside. Yawning cavernously, he regarded the three men in silence.

Brad pointed to Olaf. "Got sliced with a knife."

The Doc set his black bag on the round center table, moved the lamp into position, and laid Olaf's huge arm carefully near it. Unwrapping the bloodstained bandanna, he dropped it to the floor. He peered at the wound, made a wheezing sound, and reached for his bag.

"Is it bad, Doctor?" Olaf asked.

Doc Stebbins spoke, his voice a rusty rumble. "Hurt?"

"Little bit."

"It's more than a cut," the Doc observed. "Looks like it was hauled apart at the edges."

Sheriff McFee said dryly, "He used it when he jerked the bars out of my cell window."

The Doc looked more closely at Olaf, ran trained fingers over his bulging upper arm and across the straining muscles in his hand. "I can believe it," he announced. He looked around, his eyes as sharp as a squirrel with a mouthful of nuts.

"Where's the hot water?"

From a doorway at the end of the room, Faith McFee said, "I have it about ready, Doc."

Brad turned. He had not heard her before; he had assumed she was still asleep. But she stood in the doorway, lamplight framing her. She wore a long dress of a soft green shade that he liked, and over it a plain checkered apron. Her hair had not yet been put up, but hung in two long braids over her shoulders. She smiled at him in a surprisingly friendly fashion.

"Coffee, too," the Doc said. "We got a sick man here that needs coffee."

"Not sick," Olaf objected.

Doc Stebbins glared at him. "You want coffee, don't you?"

The word struck a responsive chord in Olaf. "Yah!"

"Then say you're sick." He looked at the girl. "Bring the water, Faith."

She did so, setting a scoured dishpan and a steaming kettle on the table beside him. He poured some of the water into the pan, tested it with a knuckle, and added the rest of the water. Lifting Olaf's hand, he plunged it in so the wound was covered. Carefully, he washed the cut, removed something from the bag that that made

Olaf growl when it was applied to his wrist, and made a neat wrapping over everything.

Faith brought the coffee. Olaf retired shyly from the light, but stayed near enough to admire his bandage. The Doc sucked noisily at his cup.

"You," he said to Brad. "I hear you tangled with Ike Quarles."

"I reckon," Brad admitted.

"In my saloon," the Doc persisted.

"He owns the One-Shot," Faith McFee explained, laughing a little at the surprised look on Brad's face.

"A man has to make a living," the Doc said defensively.

"Hope I didn't bust up your saloon," Brad apologized.

The Doc snorted. "It earned you a free beer." Setting down his empty cup, he started toward the door. "Next time hit him, and I'll give you a whisky. Maybe two." He jerked open the door and slammed it behind him.

Brad didn't know whether to laugh or not. But he noticed that neither Faith nor her uncle seemed at all amused. The door opened and Doc Stebbins put his head back in. "Come see me later, Jordan." He disappeared again.

Finishing his coffee, Brad set down the cup and reached for his tobacco. "I'll be obliged if you'll let me out of your jail long enough to work and pay my fine."

"Fine!" Faith cried. "After—after——"

"All right," McFee said wearily. "Between you and June Grant, you've beat me. Go make some breakfast, Faith. It's nigh daylight anyway."

To Brad, he said, "I'll suspend the sentence. Now, you still want a job?"

"Still," Brad said.

McFee took a chair and stretched his bare legs out.

"Miss Grant wants you to work for her. She came in last night, saying that any man who stood up to Ike Quarles was worth hiring." He paused and regarded Brad frowningly. "She can't pay much, Jordan. She ain't got much any more."

"Punching?"

McFee watched Brad roll and light a cigarette. He sighed tiredly, resignedly. "She's got more hands than she can afford now. I'd say it was for the same thing Biddle wanted—a gunhand."

"I'd like to know more about it," Brad said cautiously.

"Let her tell you," was the answer. "But you saw Quarles. And you had a run-in with the kind of men he hires. Including Biddle."

"I saw a range hog," Brad said. "A shrewd one. I was lucky twice, and he figured I was safer to have on his side than against him." His smile came out thinly. "Safer and easier to get rid of, maybe."

"That's what it'll be from now on," McFee warned him. "Getting rid of you. You hit the sore spot when you mentioned water to Biddle." He nodded vigorously. "Water's in back of it. I—— But I'll let June Grant tell you. It's her business."

He turned the subject abruptly. "You mentioned looking for a place to settle. You figure it will be here?"

"I came here for that reason," Brad said.

He could understand the sheriff's curiosity, even if he didn't like it. A man who let another man out of jail to work for someone had a right to know a few things.

Brad said, "I came for that. I haven't done anything about it yet because of Olaf. Now, from what you say, I won't be able to do anything because of this Double Q. I want to settle down in peace."

"But you're willing to start by fighting," McFee pointed out.

Brad glanced toward the door. Faith McFee stood there. He saw her thoughts clearly on her features. It was as if she were saying again, "Brutal!"

"A man has to fight sometimes," he said.

"Sometimes," she echoed. "Some men fight all the time —with no reasons."

This was between them once more. Brad could feel it like a wall that was too high to climb. Faith turned away, going into the kitchen. Without showing any expression, Brad looked once more at the sheriff.

"Where do I find Miss Grant?" he asked.

"First road west, going north out of town," McFee said. He stood up and took a turn around the room. Coming back, he stopped in front of Brad, measuring him with a penetrating gaze.

"One thing, Jordan. June Grant's a friend of mine—of a lot of people. She's got trouble. Her back's against the canyon wall now, and it don't look good for her. She needs help, but it's got to be help she can count on. You work for her Split S, you do it right or don't do it at all.

"She can't afford a man who makes a month's wages and then drifts. She can't afford a man who has his own fight and who puts that first. Work for her first and yourself afterward."

Brad studied the truculent little man in front of him. He felt his first genuine respect for the sheriff. There was a real loyalty here for this girl he spoke of.

"I earn my pay when I work," he said. "And if I take the job, it'll be the way you said."

McFee watched him intently for a moment longer. "Then come set to breakfast," he said finally.

Faith McFee was quiet during the meal, speaking only to ask one of the men if they wanted more to eat. Brad ate with appetite and, rising, he rolled a cigarette and carried his plate and cup from the restaurant where they had eaten to the kitchen. Returning, he nodded to Olaf. "Thanks for the meal, ma'am." The twinkle momentarily lighted his eyes. "It was as good as I figured."

"You're welcome," Faith McFee said, and looked away.

McFee made a show of pushing back his chair and getting up. "I'll bring your horses," he said. He went to dress.

They followed him out. Brad saddled the palomino, helped Olaf with his bay, and led both mounts from the barn. Getting aboard, he looked down at the sheriff. "I'll oblige you for my gun."

McFee went to the jail and returned with their guns and Brad's belt. Checking his gun, Brad settled it in his holster. "When I come back," he said, "I give it to you?"

"That's the law," McFee stated.

Brad took a final pull at his cigarette and rubbed it out between his fingers. He watched the tobacco flakes drift to the dusty road, and then lifted his eyes to look at the sheriff. "And what if Quarles' crew decide not to obey your law?"

Before stubbornness froze McFee's expression, Brad saw a fine line of worry. Here might be the man's true weakness; he had never been forced to test himself. He did not know how he would stand up in a fight.

"Ever had much trouble here, sheriff?"

"No," McFee said shortly.

"As I thought," Brad said. "Thanks for the hospitality."

The sheriff watched Brad follow the alley northward, with Olaf riding rigidly behind him.

"No trouble yet," McFee muttered. "But there will be. He's the kind that draws it—or goes out after it."

He turned toward the house and was reminded of Faith. Inside, he went to her. His glance was enough for her to know how he felt. Their affection for each other was deep, and she let him see it in a smile.

"He's a rough man," McFee commented. "If Quarles wants a fight, Jordan will give it to him."

"Fighting," she said bitterly.

"Your Dave Arden is supposed to be fighting Quarles," McFee pointed out.

"Dave 's careful," she answered defensively. "Quarles has too many men, too much strength." The sheriff didn't answer, and she broke out, "You don't like Dave, do you?"

"No," he told her, "I never have." He scratched behind his ear, frowning, hunting the words. "But it's your life, Faith. You're a grown woman, a thinking woman, and you do with it what you believe best."

She smoothed her apron over the green dress. Her smile was faint. "I think it best to see Dave and tell him the kind of man June has hired." She paused, adding, "Dave and Jordan won't get along. Dave is thoughtful and careful. Jordan is rash and brutal. He'll try to rush things."

"It's about time, maybe, things was rushed," McFee mumbled. "But like I said, it's your life. Ride to Dave if you want."

"No woman can put her skirts around a man to keep him safe," Faith said.

"The kind that would let her ain't worth having," the sheriff said. Going to the stove, he poured himself a cup of coffee and took it to the table. He sat down and filled his pipe, smoking in somber silence.

"Jordan's a troubled man, Faith, for all of his talk." He shook his head slowly. "A troubled man is a troublesome man. I've seen his kind before. Land-hungry, but always drifting. Never finding just what they're looking for. Because what they're looking for is always in their heads like a dream. The world's not made out of dreams. And when a man like Jordan finds that out, he's disappointed, and rides on."

Faith sighed. "Jordan is a fighter," she said slowly. "If what you said is right, June needs fighters. Maybe that's why Dave hasn't done much before: he hasn't enough fighters. Now he will have."

Her uncle regarded her quietly, feeling the bitterness in her voice, hearing the hopelessness of a woman who hated fighting and yet was coming to realize that in some cases it might be the only way.

She sounded as if she were talking to herself, putting her thoughts into words. "But Dave is no fighter. That's not his way."

McFee nodded. "That's what I've been thinking. It's like you said; Jordan and Arden won't get along at all. Jordan will ride in there full of ideas, but Arden will be his boss.

"How is it going to help June if her foreman and her hired gunhand are fighting each other instead of the Double Q?" He took a deep puff on his pipe. "Maybe I was wrong in sending him to her place."

Faith said quietly, "Yes, I think you were wrong," and went back into the kitchen.

CHAPTER NINE

IT WAS A FINE MORNING and Brad rode with his head to the breeze, getting the most of it. The air had that rare freshness of the open just before sunrise, and the dew underfoot made the grass sweet. The more Brad studied this country the more it got into him.

Some distance out of town the green hayfields began on the west. The river ran through a deep gully cut in the gentle slope that went from the valley floor up to the westerly hills. On the banks of the river Brad noticed crude rigs that were horse-drawn pumps. But those he could see were standing idle, though the hay running down from the river was yellowing from lack of water.

His was no practiced eye in irrigation. He had only seen it in Colorado and the Nebraska country, but drought alone was no newcomer to him, and it was obvious that this hay was withering from it.

At the first road, they turned west going up the easy grade until they reached a plank bridge thrown across the river. Here Brad looked down. There was no more than the trickle of water that he had seen below at the gap. Certainly not water enough to wet an acre of hay, let alone the great fields stretching to the north and south.

He glanced at Olaf now. "You got your own place to farm," Brad said. "There's no call for you to get in this fight."

"You fight, I fight," Olaf said slowly. His face twisted as he sought for the exact expression. "Partners."

"Ah," Brad said, "you still want it that way." He offered no further argument, realizing the uselessness of it. And despite Olaf's rawness to this type of life, Brad was glad to have him as a side-kick. They rode on.

The Grant house was set where a small creek came down from the mountains and rattled off to join the river. The road followed the creek in its straight line fall from the hill through the bunch grass pasture above the bed of the Sawhorse. Halfway along, Brad noticed that the water began to sink into sand until there was not even a trickle at the mouth by the bridge. But up on the knoll, where a group of resin-scented balsam poplars clustered around the house and outbuildings, there was water enough for general use. The Split S was a neat layout, but Brad's practiced eye saw signs of decay that no cowman could miss.

The bunkhouse was set not far from the kitchen door, with the big corral and barns just beyond it. One of the barns showed signs of use, but the other and a number of smaller outbuildings stood with doors gaping. It was easy to tell that this had been a big spread once, but the dry rot of bad times had struck it until it was whittled to less than a small rancher would have in New Mexico.

The house still stood fine and pretentious, and Brad could visualize the labor that had gone into its building. He got a picture of Grant coming here to homestead, making his first stake, and paying back his wife for the hardships of her life with a fine house of milled clapboards, jigsaw decorations, and many glass windows. It stood a story and a half, with a veranda running around three sides.

The yard was trampled from many years of pounding, from both horses and men, and only a little dust flared up as Brad and Olaf rode in and got down by the front door. He was no hand here yet, Brad reasoned, and so he tied the horses by the front and went up the steps to knock as a stranger would.

He glimpsed two men near the bunkhouse door as he left his horse, and another man, dusty as if he had been riding already this morning, crossing the rear yard toward the house. They were all too far away to be seen clearly. When his polite knock was answered, it was a woman who greeted him.

"You're Mr. Jordan?" she said.

She was pretty and younger than he had pictured her. Her dark eyes bright in her heart-shaped face, she stood in the doorway inviting him in. She wore her hair shorter than most women, and fixed as if she crammed a work hat on it. Her riding skirt was divided; her shirt a man's heavy one. The hand holding the door open was small but strong and calloused. She nodded to Olaf.

"Yes, ma'am," Brad said, and removed his hat. Olaf did the same and Brad led the way inside.

The parlor of the house was big and cool, and a fire in the rock fireplace was burning off the morning chill. A fat iron stove in the center of the room was cold, but it sat under its pipe with a capable look about it.

She would be capable too, Brad thought. And when she spoke, his opinion was confirmed. For all of her smallness, June Grant had a way of authority about her. "I asked Angus to let you out to work for me, if you would. Does your coming mean that you will?"

"Depends," Brad said. He was not at ease in here; the room was too large and too cold. She seemed to sense it, for she led them to a smaller room off the kitchen and seated them at a table. She brought them coffee.

"Smoke if you wish," she said. "Depends on what?"

"On what I'm to do and why," Brad said bluntly. He told her of his brush with Biddle. "That kind of work I don't like," he explained.

She had begun to frown as he talked, and now the frown deepened. "I can't meet those wages, Mr. Jordan."

"No common hand expects to work for that money, either," he said.

She picked at the edge of her shirt sleeve and rubbed it between her fingers. "I don't need common hands," she said. Her head lifted, and he saw the determination glowing in her eyes. "I dislike killing as much as the next woman, but I've waited long enough. Ike Quarles has asked for a fight, and I'll give it to him."

She met Brad's steady gaze unflinchingly. "If I lose,

I'm done quickly. If I don't fight, I'll hang on for a year or two at the most." She dropped her sleeve and put her hands together, squeezing them so that her knuckles stood out white with the pressure. "My father came here and built this place. He homesteaded the valley. When others wanted in, he let them come. He asked only for his share and no more. But he did want that, and he would fight for what he considered his."

"Your father's dead?" Brad asked.

"Three years," she said. Her voice quickened. "He helped Ike Quarles get a start. And until Jim Parker came there was no trouble. Quarles seemed content to do as the rest of us—run only as much stock as we could cut native hay for."

She stood up abruptly. "But my troubles shouldn't concern you. I'm sorry."

"Unless I work for you," Brad said quietly.

"Then you'll only be asked to do what you were hired for."

"If I work for anyone," he said firmly, "their troubles come first. I told McFee I'd work whole hog or not at all."

"I want men to fight Ike Quarles," she blurted out. "I want men who can match the hardcases he's brought in here. My men are soft; they aren't fighters. I can't ask them to fight."

That, Brad thought, was a funny way to look at it. If a man worked for a spread, that spread was his home and he should be willing to fight for it as such.

"Have you tried?" he asked.

She gave a light, quick shrug. "My foreman has questioned them. He's a good boss and he knows men. They're just punchers and no more." She paused adding, "No, I want men to fight."

"And what does Quarles want that's worth fighting for?" Brad demanded.

She led him to the side veranda and pointed to the sweep of fields visible through the hovering poplars. "Jim Parker came in here from the east," she began, "carrying a satchel full of books. We were running as many head as our winterfeed would carry. He showed us how we could get water to the land and grow alfalfa. That was four years ago, and those of us on the river and the ranches across where the creeks are heavy and run all year followed his example."

She pointed to the north. "That first ranch is Biddle's. He's Quarles' bootlicker." Her voice deepened with scorn. "Quarles is one place beyond him; his homestead runs also to the mountains and he put his cattle in the first canyons, pre-empting the land there. The river comes out of those mountains and reaches Quarles first. It drops from his north boundary to the level you see below."

The pattern came back to Brad. The world was no different on this side of the mountains. The grass was the same on one bank of a creek as on another. Men were cut of a stamp and he had found hogs from Texas to Washington.

"So," he said, "Quarles cuts off the water before it gets to you. With a dam?"

"Nothing so obvious," she explained. "The river is formed by two feeder creeks. This is odd country. The water goes underground and joins and comes out in a big spring to start the Sawhorse. Quarles and Biddle have filed water rights on the feeder creeks. Jim Parker says that we can fight them by proving that the creeks are the source of the river."

"I see," Brad said. "But by the time the Government gets through in the courts, you won't have hay or stock."

"Or land," she amended. Her face softened as she looked at the fields and at the bunch grass graze visible from where they stood. "I was born on this land. It holds my mother and father. I don't want Ike Quarles to have it—to dirty it."

She shook herself. "But I can't appeal to you that way. It isn't fair."

"You can tell me some more," Brad said. "How does filing a water right give Quarles all the water?"

"He's diverted the feeder creeks," she explained. "He had a fortunate shale slide that boxed in a canyon and created him a reservoir. All the water we get is that coming from the creeks like this one by the house. Most of them are summer dry."

"There's enough water for everybody?"

"More than enough. The north mountains are heavy with snow in the winter, and snow lies all year in some of the canyons."

"Water and land for everybody," Brad mused. He put out a hand as if reaching to feel the dirt. "It's good country." He looked down at June Grant, at the mingled despair and hope in her eyes. He made his decision. "It's worth fighting for."

Her smile was like the first sun that was starting to top the eastern mountains. And then it was gone. "If—if we lose, I can't do more than bury you."

He understood her meaning. "We'll ask no more," he said.

She turned away, walking quickly, purposefully now. "I'll let you meet the men."

"This Jim Parker," Brad said, "is he your partner?"

She looked back at him unsmilingly. "He'll be my boss it we get through this. No, Jim owns the upper end of the valley. He has less water than any of us."

"But more savvy?" Brad said, remembering what Faith

McFee had told him. "So Quarles tried to run him out."

"I can't thank you for what you did yesterday," she said.

Her voice told him what she felt toward Jim Parker. He envied the man for having a woman like this. He untied his horse, saw that Olaf was doing well, and followed her toward the rear.

The men were scattered and out of sight, but she found the one she looked for in the bunkhouse. Studiously observing the rules of a ranch, she stopped, not going in.

"Dave," she called. When a man ducked out of the doorway, she motioned to Brad and Olaf. "Here are the new men, Dave. I'll leave you to finish explaining to them." Her smile for him was warm, but with no great depth. "The men will be listening for breakfast."

She started off, and then turned. "I have a lot of faith in Dave," she told Brad.

CHAPTER TEN

AFTER June Grant had left them, Brad and Olaf followed Arden into the bunkhouse. It was a neat place, but no neater than the average man would want it. There was no sign of a woman's hand, no frills at the windows, no fancy cloth on the table that sat under the hanging center lamp. Brad had seen that kind of thing on a woman-run ranch; he was glad to find that June Grant had more sense.

The bunks were near the front with an open space at the rear. Near one side wall was the large heating stove flanked by the big table and a half dozen chairs. Brad walked past Arden and sat down; Olaf followed him.

Looking at Arden, Brad tried to reserve his judgment. He was a quick man when it came to making decisions, but now he tried to curb himself. Prepared to like Arden, to work with him in this fight, it bothered Brad to find that he could not feel the same trust in the foreman as June Grant evidently did. It was not anything he could put his finger on—Arden was amiable, smiling, a relaxed man who looked sure of himself. But the doubt was there inside Brad, not a positive distrust or dislike, but simply a lack of feeling. He could not feel drawn to Arden as he had expected.

Now he said probingly, "How strong are we here?"

Arden was standing relaxed with one hip against the edge of a bunk. He made and lighted a cigarette and then snapped the burned match between his fingers. He was no longer smiling.

"As strong as that," he said, and tossed the match out the open doorway.

Brad waited, letting Arden carry the talk, only speaking to ask a question. The men, Arden said, were of little use. There were Andy Toll and Jake Bannon and Nate Krouse. They were punchers and good enough at their jobs, but good only for those jobs. He had the same opinion of Jim Parker. A man who read too much and was no fighter for this kind of war.

Privately, Brad didn't agree with that. What he remembered of Parker had given him a different opinion. But it was only opinion, so he didn't push the matter.

When Arden turned to talking of Quarles, his voice flattened out with hopelessness. As though, Brad thought, he had about decided to give up but wouldn't say so in words. Quarles was planning to make this his big year, according to Arden, and ruin both the Split S and Parker before an injunction could force him to give up the water. Arden admitted that the Split S would have nowhere near enough hay to feed the stock through the winter. For June Grant that would mean selling all but a handful of beef at a loss. It would mean, too, that she could not meet in full her notes due at the Spokane Falls bank.

Brad shaped up a cigarette and struck a match. Blowing out the flame with a puff of smoke, he said, "What's Quarles showing in the open?"

"He's got the water tied up," Arden said.

Brad brushed the statement aside. "Until you get an injunction, that's legal," he said. "You say he's pushing the Split S. I've seen him rough Parker, but that's a different thing."

Arden moved reluctantly away from the bunk. "It's a hard thing to pin down, Jordan." He shook his head. "Quarles doesn't push June much in the open." He took a moment to flip his cigarette onto the packed, bare ground in front of the bunkhouse door, and then turned toward Brad again. "Just one thing," he added.

"Tell it," Brad said. He spoke more harshly than he intended. But if a man had something to say, he liked him to say it.

Arden shrugged. "It might not be much."

And it might be a lot, Brad thought as he listened. Arden explained that at the edge of the timber where it folded into the sage hills June Grant's father had located a fine-grassed canyon where he fattened his best stock. It was open range and belonged to him only by right of long usage. This spring Biddle and Quarles had moved in seventy or eighty head of their own prime stuff into Pine Canyon, putting the Split S back on the scantier range in the open. June had gone to Quarles with a complaint.

"He told her it was open range," Arden went on, "and said we were welcome to run his beef out if we could."

Brad nodded his understanding. It was a challenge June Grant was too weak to accept. In a way Arden was right—it wasn't too much to argue about. Open range was open range, and in a country as raw as this, the right of usage wouldn't have too much meaning.

"Even so," he said aloud, "why hasn't McFee helped?"

Arden's laugh was almost ugly. "McFee's town marshal. There's no law in the valley outside his town. No law but this." He slapped his gun.

"If that's the law," Brad said, "then we can use it as well as Quarles."

"We haven't the strength," Arden objected. "What are we against Quarles and Biddle?"

"We're no more than we want to be," Brad said. This man bothered him even more than he had at first. Signaling to Olaf, he started for the door.

"When you're ready to do something, let us know," he told Arden.

Leaving the foreman, Brad and Olaf went up to the house and entered. "Olaf and me will be at his homestead," Brad told June Grant. "There's work for us there and, until we can do something here, there's no call for all the extra feeding we'd mean to you."

June Grant looked thoughtfully in the direction of her hayfields. "It will have to be soon," she said slowly. "I can't hold out much longer." She paused and added, "I'll have a man come for you when Dave is ready."

It was on Brad's lips to ask why Arden had to wait any longer. But he stopped himself. He knew little of these people. It was not his place to work on June Grant's faith in her foreman.

He said, instead, "We'll take a boundary sashay on the way home, then," and left.

As they rode, he tried to piece together what he had learned so that it would make a coherent pattern. But there was too little to work with as yet. He had seen Quarles' kind many times. Some were slick men, and some depended on force to get what they wanted. But in every case Brad had never found a solution except to meet force with force. This was the only law certain types of men recognized.

He drew rein now on a high knoll that gave him a sweeping view of the valley. In the distance he could see Sawhorse Falls as a faint cluster of ugliness on the brown face of the flats. He remembered again McFee's position in all of this, and he wondered at a man who could draw himself into his own tight little world and let that around him shatter into pieces.

Olaf was looking, too. He caught Brad's eye and nodded understandingly. "It's a good land," he said.

"Good land," Brad agreed. "It could be a good place to live."

"Yah," Olaf said. And Brad knew that he would stick, no matter how tough the fighting got.

They reined around and rode on into the hills.

Arden watched Brad and Olaf ride off and when the first rise to the west had blotted them from sight, then he walked purposefully to the house.

June Grant was in her kitchen, getting ready for the noon meal. Arden beckoned to her, and she stepped to the comparative coolness of the side veranda.

"What made you hire a man like that?" he demanded.

Her eyes widened and a faint flush tinged her cheeks. "I hope to save my hay," she said briefly, "and my stock."

"Fight fire with fire," he murmured. His smile for her was warming, asking for inclusion in her troubles. "You've made the decision, then."

Sometimes Dave took too much for granted, June thought, but she could not help being drawn by him.

With her love for Jim Parker, she saw Arden only as a trusted friend. There was always a faint sense of warning when she felt his smile, but she put it down to a natural suspicion of anyone born with such easy charm.

"The decision was to be yours, Dave," she said. "But if you'd rather not—"

She left it there, and he looked down at her, smiling crookedly. "Hinting I might be afraid, June?"

"Or not think it wise."

"I don't," he admitted. "Quarles is too strong."

"He's not getting any weaker," she pointed out. "Is there any other way?"

Arden considered this while he took the time to roll a cigarette. He lifted it to his mouth and licked the paper. His eyes met hers. "No," he said, with complete honesty, "there's no other way."

"Then," she said with quick logic, "I couldn't do better than to hire a man like Jordan."

He laughed at her triumphant expression. "Putting it that way, you win." He touched a match to his cigarette. "Right now I'd better get to town and see to the supplies we ordered."

"That's right," she agreed. He was nearly down the steps when she called to him. "Act quickly, Dave. I think Jordan is a restless kind of man."

"Quickly, quickly," he muttered as he went to the corral for his horse. Give him two months and an army of Jordans could not do anything.

Going to the hayfields, he stopped and looked carefully at the plants. Not even two months. Unless there came a rare summer rain heavy enough to soak into the ground, six weeks would see the end of this crop. The sand here was deep and dry. Hay took a lot of moisture to stay alive through a desert summer; it needed even more to grow strong. The first cutting should be nearly ready now, he realized. Last year they had cut hay just at this time. But it had been put off this year, hoping for more growth. Well, they would have to cut, but there would be little more than stubble. There wasn't hay enough to feed more than a handful of the stock June needed to get through the winter.

He started on again, the hoofs of his horse thudding sullenly across the bridge. Arden looked down at the riverbed and frowned a little. The trickle of water in it wasn't enough to hold a small fish. And though he realized the necessity of this for his own plans, he had enough love of the soil in his nature to regret it for the moment.

At the turn he looked back, and he could see faintly two dots on the farthest bare bench. Jordan and Hegstrom, he thought, and his frown turned from regret to anger.

In Jordan he saw clearly a potential threat. Until now there had been no man in the valley with the driving strength necessary even to challenge Quarles' self-assumed leadership. One man might not seem like much, Arden thought, but it was in that very fact that the danger lay. If Quarles were fool enough to push aside the threat of a man like Jordan, Arden knew that Quarles might find himself against a wall before he realized it.

But it wasn't Quarles Arden worried about too much. Quarles had the power and the strength to handle Jordan if he awoke to his danger soon enough. It was for himself that Arden's anger turned on Jordan. He sensed in the other man a shrewdness that would force him to move more carefully. Until now, he had had it easy at the Split S; he warned himself to go more carefully.

As he rode along his anger turned to worry, and from it came a plan that took form and shape and strength. It was beautiful in its simplicity. He was Jordan's boss, wasn't he? What could be simpler than to give Jordan an order no man could live through? After all, wasn't Jordan's purpose to fight openly against Quarles?

Smiling suddenly, Arden hurried his horse. Nothing could be simpler. Nothing could be safer.

CHAPTER ELEVEN

"I LIKE TO GET the feel of the country," Brad said to Olaf.

They mounted the last bare bench, following a northwest trail, and the edge of the timber was just beyond them. Nearby, in a meadow, a few head of cattle grazed. They had the Split S brand on them, so he knew he was still on home range. Farther along and below them there was a thin razorback hill with a crest of scrub timber. It looked like a natural dividing line, and when Brad could see beyond it, the idea was confirmed. Cattle now carried Nick Biddle's odd-looking Sawhorse brand. Along with them were a few head of the Double Q.

Brad pointed out the brands to Olaf, making sure he understood their meaning. He cut due west into the timber and then along a trail that ran slightly south in its general direction. "This is all open range," he explained, "and if Grant was on it first, he's got more rights than Biddle."

He was hunting for Pine Canyon and when he found it, marked as it was by two tall ponderosas standing like sentinels at the narrow mouth, he looked back and judged he was well south of the razorback that separated Biddle from June Grant.

"But rights don't count," he told Olaf, and pointed to the Sawhorse beef grazing on the belly-deep grass.

He looked admiringly at the canyon. This was a place

to put a man's best cattle, right enough. There was water from a creek that roiled along one canyon wall, and grass deep and rich enough to keep any cow happy. It was cool in here with the high, partly timbered sides shutting out the sunlight at this hour of the day, but a notch near the end showed him where it would come in warmly in the afternoons.

Biddle and Quarles realized its value, too, that was plain. Off to one side and a short distance in from the mouth was a line shack, set above the high-water mark of the creek. Smoke rose indolently in the still air, indicating the presence of at least one person.

"We go?" Olaf wanted to know, nodding toward the shack.

"It's not time yet for trouble," Brad said, reining around. "I got other things to see first."

He followed a ridge trail that he judged would bring him north to the end of Sawhorse Valley. He rode with caution, since to his right lay Quarles' graze and Quarles' men. To the left, he caught a glimpse now and then of the jumbled mass of sage hills and rock canyons that sloped gradually toward the Columbia River. The Sawhorse was an isolated pocket on the edge of the desert, and with the railroad being built not too far away from the south gap, Brad could see its worth.

When he reached the northernmost limits of the ridge trail where a high wall of rock forced him eastward, he could look back and see the whole valley spread out below. The patches of hay meadow were like specks of green on a brown carpet, the road and its branches white threads that had been laid in a neat pattern.

"There's room for fifty," he said in a burst of anger. "But one gets rich and forty-nine starve." He studied it gloomily. "Look at it. Look at the families men could support on that land, Olaf." He sucked the tang of pine and leaf mold into his nostrils. "Timber and water and flats for grazing and hay to keep cattle fat."

He reined his horse around, and Olaf followed, contented just to be near despite the roughness of the ride.

Brad found what he was hunting before too long. He had dropped nearly to the valley floor, and now he had to work back up again. He came to the reservoir that accident had created for Quarles. Some water seeped over the jumble of boulders and trees that jammed the entrance to the deep, narrow canyon, but not enough water to do the river below much good, except when Quarles wanted to release it. It was easy to trace the water flow on up now, and Brad followed it to a great swampy meadow. Here two creeks came in, angling from either side, and both flowing strongly. They nearly filled the meadow, he saw, and seeped into the ground out of sight, later to re-form as the Sawhorse River.

It was no different from a hundred other river sources that he had seen, but it was the first one he had found so low in the hills that a man could take advantage of it as Quarles had.

This, he decided, was where Quarles and Biddle had filed their water rights. A channel had been cut across the meadow, catching a large percentage of the water before it went underground, and draining it through a cut in the canyon. Brad could hear the steady roar of a falls, and he followed the marshy ground until he could climb above it and look down on what Quarles had engineered.

The channel led the water from the canyon and over the brink of a drop to another canyon a good hundred feet below. Here it collected, straightening out and running down over rocks and brush, seeping into the earth so that its runoff was slowed until it oozed into the reservoir down below.

"He just stores it and uses it when he wants it," Brad marveled. "What gets loose is not enough to do anyone else much good down below."

A territorial or a federal court could stop this without much trouble. But nature had never waited on the slow, ponderous movements of man's laws. Hay would not stand still in its dying while a court battle was fought. And without hay June Grant would have to sell most of her stock or see them starve through the winter.

These things piled up in Brad's thoughts, and he had a new respect for Ike Quarles. The man was shrewd and clever, and Brad doubted if he had yet openly broken any law that could touch him. Quarles was a power here, but he wore no gun in McFee's town. Yet Brad knew McFee alone had no strength to stop Quarles if he chose to exert his force.

It added up to new ideas for Brad and gave him some measure of the man he was to deal with. He rode on, eastward and curving south, mulling it over, seeking a way to turn this knowledge to his own use.

The trail was long and slow, and it was past dinnertime when they came to the first spread on the east slope of the valley. A man came from the rear door of the small, solid house as they stopped. He had a friendly, open face, ruddy from sun and weather. He regarded Olaf and Brad with frank curiosity. Brad recognized him as one of the men who had helped Jim Parker from the One-Shot the day before. He introduced himself as Coe.

"You're the notorious Jordan," he said in a pleasant voice. "Light down and eat."

"Obliged," Brad said. And for a moment his hopes rose that this man might be of some help.

But once inside the roomy kitchen and introduced to the plump, heat-reddened wife of Coe, those hopes slid quickly back out of sight. There were two children, the oldest a boy of twelve or so; and an old man bent and twisted with years of living on the range. If this was what Coe had, he wouldn't be a man to chance losing it.

"You run a nice place," Brad commented when the small talk had died. Though the family was through with their meal, Mrs. Coe found food enough to heap two plates and set them before Brad and Olaf.

"Small," Coe said, "but the more a man has, the more grief he has."

Brad nodded agreement. "I see you got a fine stand of hay," he said. "You don't depend on the Sawhorse water?"

Coe's glance was quick and sharp, and the smile was gone from his eyes. "If I did, I'd have no hay," he said. "No, I was lucky. I got the only dependable creek on the east side, and when Parker showed us the new hay, I decided to try it." He waved a hand vaguely southward. "I can run three times the stock my neighbors can."

"They don't object?" Brad asked.

Coe's smile returned, but it was a different one now. "We're satisfied over here."

Brad let it drop for the time being, but after he was through eating and a decent time of visiting had passed, he rose and, with Coe and Olaf, returned to the yard.

"Looking for a job?" Coe asked.

"We're riding for the Split S," Brad said.

Coe nodded slowly. "There's no help from this side, friend. We take what we have and thank God on Sundays. We'll wait it out over here."

"You think Quarles will stop once he's got the west side of the valley?" Brad asked quietly.

"No," Coe said honestly, "a man like that never stops. Not until he's played out his string. But his way is slow. Parker has already talked of filing suit for the water. It'll do them no good over there, but he'll be hamstrung before he gets a chance at us."

"Ah," Brad said, "that's bad reasoning." He mounted his palomino and settled in the saddle. He paused to roll his after-dinner cigarette. "He lies near to you now. If they stop him from going south, he'll come east. If he can't have all that water, he'll take what he can get, and this, too. He's the kind that would take the end of the meat if he couldn't get the side."

Coe's expression showed he had never considered this before. "I'm not big enough," he said. "It's a pleasant life we have, and I'll try to keep it so."

Brad turned his horse for the road. "Quarles can see your hay from his veranda," he remarked, and led the way out of the yard.

CHAPTER TWELVE

Dave Arden put his horse behind the Sawhorse Saloon and went inside by the rear door. At the top of the stairs he followed the route Biddle had taken earlier that morning and went into the room that overlooked the street.

Ike Quarles was there, in conversation with the tall, slatbuilt Keinlan seated at a desk. Arden thumbed his hat back from his yellow hair and jerked his head at Keinlan.

"Blow, Keinlan," Quarles said. The tall man got up and, without looking at Arden, walked from the room. Arden took a seat on the sofa and rolled himself a cigarette.

Quarles said, "Well?"

"Jordan went to work for June this morning."

"She's going to fight, then?"

Arden drew deeply on his cigarette and let the smoke come out in a slow cloud. "That's what he was hired for. He's off checking boundaries now."

"What does that mean to me?"

Arden was a cautious man in some ways, but he knew when the time for carefulness was at an end. "He'll see Pine Canyon. I told him it was Grant graze before. He might want to get it back for Split S."

"He'll play hell," Quarles said. He stirred and went to the chair where the other man had been sitting. There was a humidor of cigars on the top of the desk, and he chose one, leaning back to light it. "There's three men in the line shack all the time."

"Jordan don't look like the kind to let three men stop him if he wants something," Arden remarked. He watched Quarles narrowly, waiting for a flash of expression that would tell him he had struck the right note. "We're not ready to move yet, but I can't hold him long."

Quarles savored the cigar as if this was no concern at all to him. "What if he does put Grant beef back on it? It won't be there long."

"That's your affair then. Yours and Biddle's," Arden said. "Give that kind an inch and he'll take a mile—ten miles." He looked away. "I can order him to stay away, but there's no good reason why I should."

He was watching Quarles again and saw the flicker in the fat man's eyes. "Except he might get killed."

"And you wouldn't want that?" Arden asked softly.

"I wouldn't want to be connected with it just yet." Quarles laid the cigar on the edge of a copper plate. "I'm within the law. I intend to stay that way as long as I can."

He wanted to be a big man, Arden knew. He wanted

to have the respect of people as well as power over them. It was a natural enough want. He had craved it for himself a long while.

"Just thought I'd warn you," he told Quarles. I'll do what I can to keep him quiet." He pulled a heavy silver watch from his pocket and studied it. He wanted to see Faith before she got too busy in dinner preparations at the restaurant. He got up.

Pulling down his hat, he started out the door. Quarles watched him, an odd smile forming on his heavy mouth.

When the door had shut and Arden's footsteps faded out, Quarles went to the window and looked down into the street. In a few minutes he saw Arden come back with his horse and tie it before the restaurant door. He went to the hall.

"Keinlan!" he bawled.

The tall man came back in and took his place again at the desk. "If you like my cigars so well, buy yourself a box," he said.

"You'll be glad to furnish me with cigars for life when we're done," Quarles told him. He took a turn about the room, his hands clasped behind his back, and came to a stop before the desk.

"Arden's acting edgy," he said. The blank look on Keinlan's face irritated him, and he made a gesture of impatience. "Arden is mighty anxious to get rid of this Jordan."

"Aren't you?"

"Not that anxious. Not so quick. I want you to find out why."

"How?"

"The same way you find out other things. Get Arden drunk." Quarles' tones were sharp. "I want to know, that's all."

"I'll see," Keinlan said cautiously.

"Arden might have some ideas of his own," Quarles said. "I think he's working for me. I want to know if he thinks so, too." He finished his cigar, dropped the butt on the copper plate, and lay down on the sofa. "Now be quiet. I want to sleep."

Keinlan sat silent for some time, staring at a stain on the bare board floor just beyond the desk. "By God," he muttered after a while, "who does know what Arden might be doing on his own?"

Quarles made no answer. He was breathing deeply and steadily, his massive chest and stomach rising and falling in a slow, regular rhythm. Keinlan got up and went out, not bothering to be quiet about it.

When Arden went in, the restaurant was empty except for a lone man drinking coffee. He was the gambler from the Sawhorse, and Arden nodded to him as he went to the far end of the counter. He took a stool, and when Faith came out he offered her his warm smile.

She was not responsive but brought him a cup of coffee and set the sugar and cream before him. They did not speak until the gambler left, and then Arden said:

"Something bothering you?"

Her smile was forced.

"Him?" he asked, indicating the man who had gone out. "You so ashamed of the way we feel that you hide it before other people?"

He was always putting her on the defensive, Faith thought, and she shook her head. "Just upset, I guess, Dave. About June." His look demanded further explanation, and she rushed on, not wanting to tell him of the true weight on her mind. "She was in yesterday and she's worried."

"So am I," Arden said. "Don't you think we're doing all we can?" He saw that his roughness had pushed her a little too far. She was a spirited woman, and he could sense when he had ruffled her more than she would stand. Rising, he went to her and put his arm around her shoulder.

"I'm worried, too, Faith," he said soothingly. "But we've got two new men to work with now. That helps."

"You've seen him then?"

"Who, Jordan?" He stepped back from her. "He went to work for us today."

Faith probed him, hoping to find out what she wanted to know. "And you agree to his way of doing things?"

Arden's quick mind understood what was worrying her. She had seen Jordan and realized the potential danger of his pushing them into a fight before they were ready. He saw, too, the opportunity in this.

"No," he said, "I don't agree. He's in too big a hurry."

"He's a fighter," Faith said.

Arden caught her up. "And I'm not. That's what you mean?"

"I didn't think you were," Faith said. She spoke honestly, questioning aloud. "But how can I know? How much do I know about you, Dave? Two years is a short time."

"Long enough when you know you're in love," he said.

His charm reached out and touched her. She tried to draw back from it; she wanted to think clearly now, to explain herself. But he was close, and she could feel his smile as tender as a kiss.

"Love is so many things," she said haltingly. "Just how do you feel about—about June's troubles? I don't really know. And you know everything about me."

Arden said, "June's troubles are my troubles." He

saw that it was no answer, and added, "I'm glad for Jordan's help, but he's a hurrying kind of man, and we aren't ready yet for hurry. I only hope he'll keep out of trouble long enough to be of some use to us. Is that answer enough, Faith?"

There was his smile again, hopeful and a little pleading now, asking her not to force him into a sudden decision that he might regret, asking her to let him use his own judgment. The smile was like strong words in her mind.

Her fingers reached out and traced a path down his cheek. "That'll do. It's answer enough," she said. Drawing back, she picked up his coffee cup and went to refill it. She was glad when the door slammed and the first of the early eaters came in for his meal. The need for hurry now gave her an excuse to postpone her worrying.

And with others around it was somehow easier to be with Dave. When they were alone, she often felt a vague sense of discomfort, as if his charm lay between them instead of drawing them together. When she did want to think, to analyze, it was always there. She fought against this. Once you were married to a man, you were alone with him a good deal of the time. Wanting other people around was no way to be.

Arden stayed on, eating when the dinner rush was about over, and lingering over more coffee. There were questions he wanted to ask about Jordan, hoping Faith or McFee had learned more about the man, but as yet he had had no opportunity.

He tested Faith's mood carefully when the restaurant had emptied, and he felt her withdrawal. Realizing that this was no time to probe her on the subject of Jordan, he gave her a fleeting kiss and left.

He went first to the sheriff's office and laid his gun on the desk. "Like to forget this," he said amiably.

McFee took it, grunting. His glance at Arden was curious.

Arden looked coolly back at the old man. He said, "Jordan's working for us, and Faith has no cause to worry. I think maybe I can keep him cool until we're ready."

"See that you do," McFee said shortly. "June Grant's in no position to give Quarles an excuse to jump on her right now."

Leaving the sheriff, Arden walked to the mercantile and consulted Eph Myers about the supplies that had been ordered. They should be in before a week was up, he was told, along with the mower parts he asked for. Arden was not perturbed by the slowness of delivery. Freight shipments here were a hit-and-miss proposition, often depending on Myers' going and getting the things he sold. If a man wanted things in a hurry, Myers always said, he'd better leave Sawhorse Valley and move closer to the sources of supply.

Arden paused on the board walk outside. He felt a growing irritation at Quarles. He had come today actually to see Quarles, using the talk with Myers only as an excuse. But he had got little satisfaction and no specific orders. Putting his plan into operation without coordination from Quarles was a thing he hesitated to do. For the present, he thought, it was best to work wholly with the other man. Later, when the end was closer, he could chance stepping out on his own.

Even so, he decided, it would be a good things to check on Pine Canyon and work out his plan to use it. He was not satisfied, but it was the best he could do, knowing Quarles was not a man to be rushed. He mounted his horse and turned toward the edge of the Split S graze.

Returning from Coe's place, Brad and Olaf passed near

Olaf's homestead. Brad went on, though it was getting late, following a direct line from Olaf's holdings westward. He had an idea that he wanted to check.

Stopping on the edge of the timber where Olaf had blazed trees to mark his west line, Brad pointed a long finger. "You see what I do?" he asked.

Olaf relaxed a little on his horse and peered in the direction Brad indicated. "Yah," he replied in a puzzled voice. "Creek."

Running along a flat between Olaf's timber and a rocky bluff was a deep-gullied creek. There was not much water in it, but the height of the sides and the width of the bottom told a plain story. As Brad pieced it out, at one time a lot of water had come down here.

Brad pointed again. "The other side of that bluff is Quarles' reservoir." He saw the lack of comprehension on Olaf's broad face. "I'll bet," Brad added, "this is why Quarles tried to run you out of the country. You're too close to his water system for comfort."

Understanding and excitement crossed Olaf's countenance. "One day I run my line," he said. "A man with a gun stopped me."

Brad listened attentively as Olaf described the incident, and then he followed up the line of blazed trees northward. The ridges angled slightly here, and within a hundred yards the trees ended in a jumble of giant boulders. The deep-bedded creek had swung away from them, but here it had swung back so that the homestead line cut cross it. They kept going, following the creek bed in a long curve as the horses picked their way carefully over the rocks. Finally, Olaf pointed to a stake. "Corner," he said.

Brad looked back, trying to sight due south. Because of the great masses of rock and a hill in the way, they had come the last two hundred yards in an arc rather than along the line. But, drawing the line with his eye back to the point where they had left it, he saw where the trouble lay.

He turned to Olaf with a wide grin. "No wonder a man with a gun turned you back. Your west line cuts right down the middle of that meadow where Quarles starts the water into his reservoir. He wants you out of the country for good!"

"Yah?" Olaf questioned.

"Sure," Brad said excitedly. "You got no more right to all the water than he has. But once you file that homestead and come back to prove it up, you can keep him off there. You could fill in his ditch and turn the feeder creeks back where they belong." He paused. "How'd you run that line, Olaf?"

"Compass," Olaf said.

Brad remembered that Olaf had been mate on a sailing ship. If he knew navigation, he would know how to run a simple line like this. "That," he said, "clears up a lot of things."

He worked the horses down to the meadow, and tried to get an approximate position there as to where Olaf's line ran. He had about figured out that Olaf owned the east third of the meadow, when the sound of a hoof on rock jerked his head up.

In a moment, two riders burst through the lower end of the meadow, pushed across the place heavy with seepage, and headed straight for him and Olaf. Brad recognized the great bulk of Ike Quarles, and with him was Newt. When they got within speaking distance, Brad had his rifle in plain sight across his saddle horn.

"The drifter!" Quarles said.

"I'm about through drifting," Brad said slowly. "I was thinking about taking up a homestead."

Quarles sat very still in the saddle, both hands clenching the reins tightly. Newt, at his side, stirred. But a low word from Quarles held him back.

"Not here you don't," Quarles said.

Brad had made his statement as much to get a rise out of Quarles as anything else. Now he saw the possibilities of his own talk. "Why not?" he demanded. "It's government land. Why, I could drain this meadow, and both me and Olaf would have some mighty good hayfields."

Quarles spoke quietly, without emphasis, but the very lack of it sent a cold warning along Brad's spine. "Not here," he said. He shifted his weight, the saddle creaking protestingly. "There's plenty of land down below for both you and the Swede. Take that, and stay out of these mountains."

"That an order?" Brad asked.

"An order!"

Brad's voice was still cool. "Like the one Biddle tried to give me this morning?"

"Biddle's a fool. I'll make you the same proposition with better terms." Quarles' calculating gaze measured Brad, seeking a chink in his armor.

"I never liked to work for a loser," Brad answered. "I'll stick with the Split S."

He could see it hit Quarles, doubling his caution. Quarles would be smart enough to know Brad was not the kind to make an idle boast. He would think Brad had a plan. And that was what he should think.

Quarles stirred again and reined his horse around. "You're through here, Jordan. Get out while you can."

"Like Parker did?" Brad asked mockingly.

Quarles raked his spurs hard against his horse and rode off, taking Newt with him. Brad watched until they were out of sight. Quarles had left easily enough, but only because he held the upper hand for the moment. Brad put his gun in the boot. Because Quarles had backed away didn't mean he was through. Brad knew his kind. Quarles would never be through until he destroyed everyone opposing him—or destroyed himself.

CHAPTER THIRTEEN

IN THE WEEKS that followed Brad grew restless. Olaf took the waiting philosophically, spending the time in improving his homestead. Brad helped him, though he had no genuine liking for that kind of work. But it was something to pass the time, and now that was what seemed to matter.

Finally he rode to the Split S. Quarles was being altogether too quiet to suit him. Even though Quarles was a shrewd, careful man, who walked the tightrope of the law, he was not the kind to take the taunts Brad had flung at him.

Bluntly Brad pointed out to June Grant that the silence coming from the Double Q was unnatural. He was afraid there was more behind it than just caution. "Quarles," he told her, "might be needing time to help him out. If that's it, then we ought to hit him before he's ready."

"I've spoken to Dave," she said. The frown of worry Brad had noticed before was deeper than ever. "In a thing like this there can't be more than one boss. He's hired to do it, and so I'll go along as he says."

"And I'll go along with you as I promised," Brad said.

"Not if you feel otherwise," she returned.

He made no answer, though the temptation was great. His promise was as strong as his inner loyalties. If that needed explaining to her, let someone else do it.

"I'm staying," was all he said.

The relief she felt was plain on her face. He could not see why, when she was so keyed up with waiting and watching her hay shrivel before her eyes, she would be so patient with Arden. But he had agreed to abide by what she said.

"We have to let him make the first move," she explained. "As Dave says, the Split S must be in the clear when this is over. We'll have no one say that I started a range war."

Fine, Brad thought, but maybe there wouldn't be any Split S to say it about. But all he said was, "Send for me when you're ready."

He rode back slowly, refusing her invitation to eat with them. It was growing dusky as he followed the flats toward the far end where a sharp trail led up to Olaf's meadow and on to his house.

June Grant, he felt, was putting too much trust in Arden's judgment. And yet what else could she do? A woman alone needed a man to turn to and, outside of Jim Parker, there seemed to be no one but Arden. She had explained to Brad that Parker was in no position to do anything. He was new to this kind of country, unfamiliar with guns and fighting, and there was little chance that he would get anything but a bullet for his pains. He had wanted to help her, she admitted, but her fear of his getting hurt had forced him into a promise of waiting.

As Brad came to the sharp trail rising through the timber, he turned his mind to riding. It was darkening here under the trees, and the palomino needed what help he could get to make the steep, rocky pitches.

Finally Brad came to Olaf's field and the last of the daylight eased the strain somewhat. He was nearly across it when he heard a sharp, keening cry of anger from the direction of the cabin. He reined in the horse and squinted that way. But the gloom and the trees hid everything from sight. He put the horse in motion, going in at a steady run.

When he was nearly to the end of the field, a bullet whined out of the darkness ahead and nicked the grass near him. He reined the horse to the left, making a zig-zagging trail until he hit the edge of the timber on the west side. A second bullet missed, and then he was out of sight in the trees.

Without slowing, reckless of the dark now, he sent the horse along a narrow deer trail. Tree branches reached out, slapping them both, but Brad paid no attention. He could visualize what had happened, and anger welled in him. They had waited until he was gone and then closed in on Olaf.

He reached the clearing around the cabin, the horse moving cautiously now, his hoofs padded by the forest duff. Brad left the saddle, ground-reining the palomino, and slipped forward on foot. He could hear men not far away, and the harsh voice of Newt rose in an order.

"Watch for him! Watch for him!"

Brad slipped up behind the bole of a thick cedar. There in front of the cabin were four horses. Someone spoke from inside the cabin, and Newt answered from the doorway. That meant two men were prowling out-side. Brad left the shelter of the tree, and at that instant Newt saw him.

Brad fired, but his angle was bad, and Newt was in the shadow of the building. He heard his bullet thud into wood. Newt's answering shot buried itself in a tree near him. Brad charged, seeking a clearer aim. He felt a root under his foot and he pitched forward off balance. The movement saved his life as a rifle butt crashed down from behind, aiming for the space where his head had been, and driving with numbing force into his shoulder.

He kept on going, face into the dirt, his gun flying from his hand. When he tried to twist as he fell, the rifle butt came down again, catching him above the ear. The sensation of warm blackness enfolded him. He reached up to push it away, but he had no strength, and he had to stop fighting.

He awakened with a ringing head and the feel of icy water on his face. He was in the cabin, half propped in his own bunk. He saw Olaf across the way, his round, usually good-humored face bleeding from half a dozen bruising blows, and one eye closing rapidly.

By the door the lanky cowboy Clip stood with a gun. One shoulder was still bandaged, but there was no mistaking the way he juggled the gun in his good hand. He was not too shot up to use it. On the other side of the room stood a man with a rifle. He was a wizened, bow-legged man that Brad had never seen before. But he had seen the stamp that was on all his kind, and Brad knew that here there would be no mercy.

Newt and a fourth man stood near Brad. Newt had the water dipper in his hand. In his eyes there was the pale desire of one born to cruelty. "He's awake," he said.

Brad put both hands tentatively on the edge of the bunk. The pain went up his right shoulder, but he could stand it. Blinking his eyes to force away the last of the dizziness, he threw himself forward. From the other bunk he caught a blur of movement as Olaf, beaten as he was, tried to throw himself off the bunk. There was a rafter-shaking crash as he fell to the packed earth floor.

Brad thought that his quickness was still in him. But with absurd ease Newt stepped aside, letting him go by. With a low laugh Newt brought the dipper down across the back of Brad's neck. Brad lit on Olaf's out-stretched body with one shoulder, rolled, and came groggily to his knees.

Newt's eyes gleamed again and he dropped the dipper, stepping in. Brad got to his feet and swung. Newt missed stepping aside, and the force of the blow sent him reeling against the man nearby. Brad charged and a foot came out, tripping him and sending him to the floor again. Newt's laugh had changed to a curse as he drove the toe of his boot against Brad's ribs.

Brad shook his head and tried to get up again. He made it to his knees when Newt's foot again caught him. He felt the hardness of heavy leather against his chin—and then the smothering blackness once more.

Again they brought him around, and this time Newt took no chances. Brad was propped against the wall, his arms roped, and Newt went deliberately to work.

"You're leaving, you hear, you? You and the Swede are leaving." Newt was laughing again as his fists methodically worked over Brad's face. From the floor Olaf groaned and struggled almost to his feet before the lanky cowhand walked over and contemptuously kicked him down again.

"You drifters know only one kind of talk," Newt said savagely. "This!" And his knee drove up brutally. Brad managed to turn, taking it on the hip instead of in the groin. He sucked in a breath and sent blood and spittle into Newt's face.

Brad kicked forward, putting his back against the wall, and driving his head into Newt's belly. He had the satisfaction of hearing a grunt of pain. And then Newt was down under him. Brad tried to beat the man with his head, throwing it until he felt as if his neck would snap.

"Get him off!" Newt yelled.

A hand got Brad by the collar and jerked. Newt came up swearing and lashed out with his fist. Brad felt the blow on his mouth, and he spat again. Newt threw a leg, tripping him, and, as he fell, Newt kicked a third time.

Brad felt his ribs give, and then all breath, all conscious-ness, left him.

This time when he came around the rough jolting of a horse beat at his bruised body. The ropes were still on him, with others holding him in the saddle. After a few minutes he found strength enough to look around. Olaf was roped in the same manner on his little bay. On either side of them the Double Q men rode easily. Ahead Brad could see nothing, but when he turned his neck, he caught a glimpse of the town lights behind. The pain of movement was too intense and his head dropped forward.

It was too great an effort to open his eyes, and so he kept them shut, sensing where they were by the coolness of the air and the pitch of the road underneath. He knew when they came to the summit of Knothole Gap, and he knew when they had started down the other side.

A short distance down, Newt's voice came briefly, "Quirt 'em the rest of the way!"

The palomino jerked forward as rein ends slashed his rump. Brad opened his eyes now to see the pitching dark-ness ahead blur into his face. The palomino was sure-footed and, despite his fright, kept his balance. Brad tried to talk and succeeded only in forcing out a croak. But after a time he got control of his voice, and the horse slowed under the familiar sounds.

Finally he had the animal halted, and he slumped in the saddle, unable to move. He listened for sounds from above, but all he could hear was the scrabble of hoofs below. Olaf, he thought, and wondered how long the rickety bay pony could last.

He urged the palomino on then, using his knees to direct it Indian fashion. Where the gap met the main wagon road, he found Olaf and the bay. The horse was spent, head hanging, unable to travel farther. Olaf sagged in the saddle like a great mound of earth. But when Brad rode up, his voice was clear.

"They beat me, Brad. I got you beat, too."

"We're not beat," Brad said. The pent-up rage of what had happened blurred his voice. "Once we get loose we're not beat, Olaf."

He went to work with what strength he could muster, shifting the the ropes, seeking a way of loosening them. But Newt was a clever man with a hitch, he discovered, and the more he worked the tighter they got. Olaf had no better luck. And finally Brad was forced to stop.

"Can that horse go at all?"

"I'll try," Olaf said. He sounded as if he were growing weaker.

"Use your knees," Brad directed. He worked the palomino behind the bay and, finally, the smaller horse started under their combined efforts. Slowly, doggedly, they got it going up the long grade to the top of the gap.

More than once Brad thought the bay was completely done, but from somewhere it mustered strength enough to pull the grades, until at last as dawn cracked the eastern darkness, they stopped in front of Tim Teehan's place.

Brad shouted, but his voice was drowned in the sound of water running into the basin. He shouted again, and Olaf's bellow joined him. He kept shouting until his throat seemed scoured raw, and at last there was a light through a window and the door came open.

Tim Teehan came out holding a lantern high. When he saw the two men, angry sounds burst out of him. "Double Q!" he said bitterly.

"Double Q," Brad managed to answer. He felt Teehan's hesitation. "If you're afraid of them, just cut us loose."

A tall woman in a flowing wrapper came out to stand

beside Teehan in the lantern light. Her gasp ran over Brad and Olaf. "The poor boys! And you stand there, Tim Teehan!"

"Double Q did it, Molly."

"Double Q be damned!" she cried. "Go get a knife, you old fool!"

Brad smiled faintly and slumped forward. He would have pitched from the saddle had not the ropes held him tightly.

CHAPTER FOURTEEN

Brad struggled back to warm sunlight and a feeling of lassitude fighting against the aches in his body. He opened his eyes and saw Olaf seated in a chair near him, smoking his foul pipe. Olaf's face looked like a ripe, bruised peach.

"We made it," Brad said.

"Yah," Olaf answered. His smile came as he saw that his friend was awake. "The lady says all right." The smile left him, and Brad saw something in the round face that had not been there before. Bitterness had come to Olaf and it had hardened him visibly.

The tall woman Brad remembered opened the door and bustled in. She carried a basin of warm water and, when she saw Brad was awake, she set it down and went to him. She was more than tall. She was huge. She would have made three of Tim Teehan with some left to spare. But for all that she moved gracefully, and when she touched his sore body her fingers were gentle.

There was the lilt of Ireland in her voice when she spoke. "And how might you be feeling now?"

"Hungry," Brad said.

"Your friend got that way yesterday," she said, "and he's up and about already." She bustled out.

"Yesterday!" Brad said to Olaf.

"Yah," Olaf agreed. "It's three days now."

Brad lay back, shutting his eyes. Three days! It was three days more before he found himself a whole man again. But once he had awakened, his strength returned rapidly. Molly Teehan's food was good and nourishing, and Brad had a constitution as strong as Olaf's. Once he was up and walking, he made good progress.

From Olaf he learned the details of Newt's coming. Olaf had been splitting firewood when they had ridden up. The sound of his ax had dulled the noise of their approach, and they had thrown a loop on him before he could move.

"I break the rope," Olaf explained. "One man hit me with a gun. That broke." He shrugged and his face clouded in memory. "But they are four. I get beat."

And so they were run out, Brad thought. Their gear would have been disposed of, and who was to say they had not thought better of things and left the country. Quarles was shrewd and had not chanced a killing on his hands.

Now Brad felt strong enough to travel, and he told Molly Teehan so. "I'd like to pay," Brad said.

"Pay!" She put her hands on her hips and glared at him. " 'Tis Double Q you ride against, isn't it? Pay!"

Tim Teehan put in a cautious appearance. "Faith McFee was up the day before you came. You're riding for Split S. That's pay enough."

Brad thanked them, and he and Olaf went out to their horses. They had been given good care, and even the bay looked fairly fit. Saddling, Brad mounted slowly. His body still pained him, and the wrapping Molly Teehan had put on his ribs made his movements none the easier. But he found pleasure in the feel of a saddle.

The Teehans came to the door. "If you need help," Molly Teehan cried, " 'tis here."

Brad saw the withdrawal on Tim Teehan's face, and so he only waved, and reined toward Sawhorse Valley. From Molly he would find help, he knew. But her husband was like McFee, a man afraid of cutting short the last of his life.

They rode slowly in the morning sun, down the trail to the flats and along to the town. They had no guns, and so there was no reason to stop at the sheriff's office. Instead, Brad drew up before the mercantile and dismounted stiffly.

There was no more than a handful of people on the street—but as one they stared as Brad and Olaf rode up and stopped. The blacksmith's boy left the livery at a quick run, darting off to carry the news.

So their going had got around, Brad thought, as he went into the store. He came out, his money belt flatter, but with a pile of goods on the freight dock waiting for him. At the livery, he rented a team and wagon, saying no more than he had to. Jube's father required a deposit on the horses and wagon.

"Might get hurt in the hills," he explained.

Brad took it as meant and paid. When the goods were loaded, he and Olaf climbed onto the wagon and started off, the saddle horses tied behind. Faith McFee ran out, calling to them, and Brad stopped.

She came up to the wagon, her face flushed with heat from the cookstove. "I just heard," she said. "It's almost dinnertime, and the restaurant is open."

"Eat," Olaf said in a pleased voice. Brad turned the

team and silently put the wagon alongside the restaurant. He and Olaf followed Faith inside.

Brad did not want to take the time for this. But besides not wanting to antagonize the girl, his common sense told him that it might be a good idea to find out a few things that had happened while he and Olaf were gone.

It was still too early for the regular diners and, for the moment, they had the place to themselves. Faith put soup, thick with beans, in front of them and added generous slices of bread. Olaf dipped in at once. Brad waited, watching the girl.

"I heard you'd left the Sawhorse," she said. Her eyes lingered on the bruises still mottling Brad's face. It was too tender yet to run a razor over, but she seemed not to notice his crop of reddish whiskers. "Now I understand."

"Then the news got around that we'd gone?" Brad asked.

"Dave Arden brought it," she answered. "He rode to see you four or five days ago and everything was gone."

"So I thought," Brad nodded.

Just then the dealer from the Sawhorse Saloon walked in. He stared for a while at Brad and Olaf, and then quietly took a seat. Addressing Faith, he said casually, "Nick Biddle just rode out. He's been in town an hour."

"Thanks," she said, and took his plate to him. When she looked again at Brad he was eating, a faint smile on his face.

"That goes for me, too," he murmured to her.

"You were foolish to come to town like this," she said softly. "Biddle and Quarles will have men over there before you get back."

"So I figured," he said.

She gave up all pretense. "Must you go back?"

"I have a score to settle," Brad said quietly. His eyes flickered. "So does Olaf."

"Is it worth another beating to settle a score?" she cried. She saw the dealer looking at her, and she fought to lower her voice. "Or more?"

"More this time," Brad agreed gravely. "The news is out. If Quarles does anything to us, he'll have to break the law openly this time. He'll order us shot."

"And you're willing!"

"To take a chance?" He nodded. "He made a mistake. Or Newt did. It was foolish for them to think we would keep running." As he lifted his coffee cup, he felt the wrapping over his ribs pull. "Or they thought we were too beat to come back." He shook his head and the faint, cold smile she had seen the day he roughed Newt was on his lips. "Quarles can't afford to make mistakes."

Others came in then, and she turned her attention to serving them. Brad and Olaf seemed to be objects of curiosity but, outside of casual nods, the men carefully refrained from taking open notice of them. It was, Brad knew, the safe way to act. If ever a showdown came, the ones who had displayed friendship would be pointed out by others.

Finally there was a lull. Brad had waited patiently until he could speak to Faith again. Now he said, "How was the news taken?"

"June Grant thought——"

"I can guess what she thought," he interrupted. "What about the sheriff?"

"He thought you'd run, too."

"They all would," Brad agreed. He reached for his money, but she refused it. Thanking her, he and Olaf went back to the team and wagon. Brad directed the horses onto the road north.

"Get guns out now?" Olaf said, as they passed the town limits.

Brad squinted into the distance. There was no sign of

anyone except a few men that he could faintly see working at cutting native grass hay off to the east.

"Good a time as any," he said.

Olaf delved into the supplies in the wagon bed and
came up with two .44's and two carbines. Brad put his
.44 in the holster and the carbine on the floor at his feet.
He wished for the familiar feel of his old guns back.
With a new .44 or carbine a man never knew how they
would shoot, and this was no time to have to learn the
eccentricities of a weapon.

Olaf sat with his carbine held loosely across his knees.
In his eyes and on his face was the look Brad had first
noticed at Teehan's. Sometimes there was the old pleasure
in Olaf's smile, but more and more of late Brad had seen
this grimness creeping up on him so that now he rode
with his eyes sharp, squinting into the distance.

"We'll go home now," Olaf said.

Brad hesitated a moment. That had been his idea
until he had talked to Faith in the restaurant, but now
he decided against the move. "Not yet," he said. Looping
the reins over the whipstock, he rolled a cigarette, holding
the paper between his legs to cut off the slight wind
rippling the air.

"That's where they'll expect us," he said. "It might be
a good idea to go to the Split S first."

Olaf studied that, and Brad realized that for the first
time Olaf had an active, understanding concern of things
in this valley. "So. Good," Olaf agreed.

At the turn Brad noticed the hay on either side. It was
still uncut though, as he last remembered it, some could
have been salvaged by cutting. As it stood now it was a
strong yellow and beginning to turn brown at the edges.
He looked disgustedly up toward the ranch. If Arden was
not willing to make a fight, the least he could do was to
save what he could for June Grant.

Brad's irritation grew as, from the bridge, he could look out and see the great stacks of first cutting Biddle and Quarles had built up. And already there was promise of second cutting showing green on their hayfields.

Going into the yard at the Split S, he left the team by the rear door, and went up to the kitchen. Olaf stayed on the wagon seat, the rifle still lying across his knees.

It was June Grant who let Brad in, and the coolness he saw in her face vanished as she became aware of the marks of the fight still on him.

"So that was it!" she said. She threw the door open. "Come in, both of you." There was a surge of hope plain in her voice. As if, Brad thought, his coming had renewed her faith in something.

"That was it," Brad said soberly. He signaled to Olaf. The big man made no move; he was looking across the fields as though he were seeking something.

"Olaf, coffee!" June Grant cried. And reluctantly Olaf climbed from the wagon and came into the house.

She poured it for them, took a cup for herself, and sat with them at the kitchen table. She waited expectantly. "I see," Brad said to her, "the hay's gone for good."

"Dave's been trying," she said defensively. "First the old mower needed parts. And then when they came, the frame broke apart. We had to order a new machine."

Brad scratched at the wiry red beard he had grown. "Some of your neighbors across the valley should be through cutting by now. Coe, for instance. Or isn't this borrowing country?"

"It used to be," she said, "when Dad was alive." There was a faint flush creeping up her cheeks. "You're just the same, Brad. Do you take a delight in badgering me?"

He noticed her use of his first name, and took it as an acceptance of his presence that had been missing before. "I like to get things done," he said. "Maybe Arden never thought of it. You might try, though, and at least get that cut and out of the way."

He shifted the subject, feeling that it was disposed of. "I'd better tell you that my being here might make Quarles move in."

"I know that," she said.

"It'd be best if we went then," he said.

She answered as Faith had. "Must you go back?"

"I've got a score to settle," he told her.

Her answer came in the words he wanted, though he had held small hope of hearing them. "Then settle it here!" Her head lifted defiantly. "After what they must have done—what it looks like they did——"

"Beat us up and drove us off," he said shortly.

"There's no good in waiting longer," she finished.

"It's up to Arden, isn't it?"

He saw the flush again. "When Dave hears, he'll be willing," she stated flatly.

"Unless," Brad said, "he's afraid of this same thing happening to you. Quarles ran us out because we were close to the water up there. He might figure it's a good way to get you over and done with. He's about where he can't wait much longer."

"It won't happen to me," she said. "And what is a little more grief, anyway, if it means a chance of saving something?"

Something, he thought. She no longer hoped to save it all—just some part of it. He stood up. "In that case," he said, "I'll see to the team and wagon."

Brad and Olaf ran the wagon into the big, unused barn, and made their beds close by it. The team they put in the other barn where there was still a little hay and feed from the winter before. That done, Brad made up two packs such as men could carry behind a saddle and use to camp in the open. The supper call came before he was finished, and when he went to the house, he saw that Arden had come in and was at the table. June Grant stepped to the door.

Brad said, "We ate big in town, and I've got more to do. We'll set in after the rest are done."

She nodded, and Brad went back to the barn. The hunger of a man still healing was strong in him when he started for the house again. Olaf walked along beside him saying nothing, and with the wary look still about him.

CHAPTER FIFTEEN

T HE MEN were still at the table, but nearly finished, and Brad stood just inside the door waiting. He had met the three Split S hands before, but so casually that there had been little chance to study them. Now he looked at them carefully and hopefully, but it took little time for him to realize that what he sought was not here.

They all glanced at him, then returned quickly to their eating. By their acceptance of his and Olaf's presence, Brad knew June Grant had prepared them.

Andy Toll was tall and lank, loose in the joints, and with the quiet smile of a man without brains enough to know when he was in danger. He acknowledged the greeting to Brad and Olaf with indifference. Jake Bannon and Nate Krouse reacted differently. And it was to them that Brad turned his interest. Of the two, Bannon was the younger and seemed to offer more encouragement— if any was to be had. He was a settled man in his thirties, but there was a light in his eyes that Brad had seen in others. Settled or not, men like that could only be pushed so far. Brad did not relish this kind when the chips were down. Too often a sudden recklessness could ruin things. But, even so, Bannon was worth more than a satisfied hand like Andy Toll.

Nate Krouse was a gray-haired veteran of many a range drive. It was stamped on him, as though the dust and grime from Texas to Montana had ground deep into his weathered skin. Yet in him, too, there was something lacking. It was not any particular thing that Brad could put a finger on, but it was there—a feeling of emptiness in the man. He would have no drive left, and few desires. This was his home now, and he would ask only to be left alone to run out the rest of his life in peace.

Andy Toll chose to begin a conversation as he forked pie into his weakly smiling mouth. "Something ripped up three rods of fence in the north pasture, June. We found it this morning. Looked like grizzly work."

Nate Krouse snorted his disgust. "A grizzly or men. And there wasn't no grizzly tracks around."

Arden said, "Were there man tracks?"

"Hard ground," Krouse answered. "Close clipped grass that's been trampled. I couldn't see any sign at all."

"So it could have been a grizzly!" Andy Toll announced. He looked with pleased triumph around the table.

"You'd rather it was," Jake Bannon said sourly. He had a harsh face, whiskered nearly to the eyes. It was strangely emotionless, so that most of his expression lay in his eyes.

"Stop that!" June Grant ordered. The weariness in her voice told Brad this had gone on before.

He looked now toward Bannon, measuring him. He got a full stare in return. "You figure it was Nick Biddle, Bannon?"

"I figure so," Bannon said quietly. "If it was, he won't stop just because we fixed up a piece of fence."

Dave Arden was sitting silently at his place. Brad glanced his way quickly, and saw that Arden's hands had a piece of bread nearly squeezed in two. But whatever was upsetting him, he was saying nothing about it. Brad probed Bannon further, watching Arden as much as the man he spoke to.

"You think he'll come back soon?"

"He ain't hurried before," Bannon said. "He's working on us slow. We can't make no tally this time of year. When we do start the roundup he'll have plenty of time to cut us down short."

Arden spoke then, his voice jerky. "We can't prove that."

Bannon looked at him in faint surprise. "I don't need to prove it," he answered. "Our fence lays against those gullies of his that work into the rimrock. Once the stock is in them, it ain't found easy—but that don't mean he didn't move it there."

Krouse took it up, talking as much to Brad as to Arden. "Cougar losses run high some seasons. There's cougars in them hills. If we yell short tally, Biddle can always blame them."

"He can't get our beef out of the valley," June protested. "What good would it do him?"

"I've seen more spreads busted by draining off the stock slow than were ever hurt by big rustlers," Brad answered. "If Quarles wants to weaken you, this is one way of doing it. Even if he ran the cattle into the mountains and left them to starve, you'd be out that much sooner."

Andy Toll raised unbelieving eyes to Brad. "That ain't human," he objected.

Arden pushed back his chair. "If you men are right," he said, nodding toward Krouse and Bannon, "then it's time to do something. That means Quarles has started in on us." He headed for the door. "I'm going to do a little looking myself."

Brad said dryly, "Want help?"

"I'll make it easier alone," Arden answered shortly, and walked out.

Brad grinned faintly. Nate Krouse made another snorting sound. "Means Quarles had started in on us," he repeated after Arden. "He's been on us for a year now!"

"Not openly," June said.

"This ain't open, either," Krouse reminded her. "And it ain't the first time we had fence cut." He got up, muttering about mending saddle gear, and went out the door. Bannon followed him at once. Brad rolled a cigarette and smoked thoughtfully.

It didn't make sense the way Arden had acted. Krouse's news had upset him a lot more than a man accustomed to such things should get. And if it had happened before, Brad could see no reason why Arden should choose this particular time to make an investigation. Brad started out on the impulse that not all was right.

"Don't hold supper," he said abruptly. Nodding to Olaf to come along, he went to the bunkhouse. He found Krouse sitting crosslegged in tailor fashion and working on a piece of bridle. Jake Bannon was smoking by the stove and throwing cards down in a desultory game of solitaire. Both men looked up.

Brad said, "What's the matter with Toll?"

"He don't like to think bad things," Bannon said heavily. "They bother him. He don't like to be bothered, so he don't think."

If there was any humor in Bannon's words, Brad failed to appreciate it. He had seen too many men follow the same path. "How would you handle that busted fence?" he asked suddenly.

Bannon tossed a red queen on a black king. "Wait and see."

"Seems to me you've been waiting quite awhile."

"We take orders from Arden, the same as you," Bannon

pointed out. He turned his back, closing off the conversation. Krouse had nothing at all to offer.

Brad said, "I think I'll do a little looking myself."

Krouse looked up. Bannon made no move except to toss down another card. It was Krouse who spoke. "Help yourself," he said.

Brad turned and went out. Olaf followed and helped saddle. Under Brad's painstaking work while at the homestead, Olaf had come a long way in his handling of cowhand chores. He saddled expertly, and he could put on a pack with a diamond hitch as well as the next man. A little shooting practice with the gun Brad had given him, as well as with a rifle, had brought results.

They mounted now, and Brad glanced toward the light spilling yellow out of the open bunkhouse door. "Olaf," he said, "never get satisfied. And never think when you hire out that your work is done because the sun sets."

"Yah," Olaf agreed. "Foolish. When they fight, it's too late."

"Always too late," Brad repeated softly.

He reined northwest into the high pastureland. The night was not yet full dark, but a deep, dusky twilight that gave odd shapes to the jagged hills and the trees along the twisting creeks of the uplands. Stopping on a knoll, he could see a pair of lights some distance ahead. One would be Biddle's, the other Quarles'.

While he watched, something came between him and the first light; and the something was not too far off. By listening closely, he made out the drum of hoofs on the hard-packed earth.

"Rider," he said. "Now who's fool enough to break his neck hurrying in the dark?"

"Arden going to see Quarles," Olaf said from beside him.

Brad swung his head. "What for?"

Olaf's shrug was faintly visible. "I saw his horse there, two—three times."

It was on the edge of Brad's tongue to ask Olaf why he hadn't spoken of this before. And then Brad realized that to a man strange to the country, much of what went on had been incomprehensible. The ways of the cattle-land were not things that Olaf could understand easily.

Brad only said, "Let's mosey along and find out."

CHAPTER SIXTEEN

ARDEN RODE NORTHWEST across the upper Split S range to make it appear as if he were going to investigate the downed fencing. Once out of sight and earshot of the ranch, he swung across Biddle's graze.

It was almost full dark by the time he put his horse into Quarles' yard. Newt came from the bunkhouse, and Arden gave his name. This display of caution struck him as curious.

Inside the house he found Quarles smoking a cigar, relaxed in an easy chair. Arden said, "What's Newt doing on guard?"

"The drifter and the Swede came back." Quarles' eyes measured Arden. "That's what you came to tell me?"

"One of the things," Arden said. "They're staying at Split S."

"So I figured," Quarles said, "when they didn't show at the homestead."

Arden took a nervous turn around the room and then, realizing that Quarles was watching him too closely, he forced himself to calmness. "Running them out that way was a fool thing to do," he blurted.

Quarles' eyebrows went up. "I didn't want that drifter around," he said. "He was getting too close to things."

"Then you should have got rid of him for good," Arden countered.

Quarles smoked in silence for a moment. His deep-sunk eyes were thoughtful as he saw the nervousness Arden could not conceal. Finally, he said, "I like to stay within the law as long as I can."

Arden silently cursed Quarles' unperturbed control. "You can't any longer," he said.

"Not much longer," Quarles agreed. He brushed smoke from in front of his face and apparently dismissed the subject. "What else did you have to tell me?"

"Biddle's rustling Split S stock again," Arden accused hotly.

"Putting his brand on it?" There was a jeer in Quarles' question.

"My brand goes on all Split S beef," Arden said. "That's the deal."

"See Biddle, not me," Quarles told him. A smile pulled down the corners of his heavy mouth. "Maybe he's just holding it for you."

Fury welled up in Arden. He paced around the room, working it all over in his mind. When he faced Quarles again, he said, "I don't trust Biddle."

"He's handy to have around."

"For a while, maybe," Arden admitted. His voice dropped, coming slyly. "But he's about through. He's got almost as much graze as you have. He's got good meadows in the hills."

Quarles lifted his hand and rapped ash from his cigar. "I'll take care of Nick when the time comes."

"And Jordan?" Arden flung at him.

"You're edgy," Quarles observed, and waited.

"He's ready to move," Arden told him. "And from the way June acted tonight, he's about got her convinced I'm stalling."

"You don't play it smart," Quarles answered. "You're getting spooky."

Brad and Olaf cut across Biddle's land in a long arc, going through a gate far up the Split S fence and following unfenced Sawhorse range until they could drop down toward Quarles' place. No one molested them; there was no sign of life except the bunches of bedded-down cattle they passed. But as they approached the Double Q, Brad made doubly sure and walked his horse softly. Nearing the buildings, he left Olaf with the horses on a rise and slipped forward on foot.

The big Double Q bunkhouse was spilling over with noise as Brad cut a wide path around it. He came up to the house on the far side, cautious against meeting a dog, but there seemed to be none. Once he heard a horse nicker nearby, and it took him a moment to realize that it was tied in front. He slipped quietly up to it.

His hand touched the animal's neck soothingly and his soft words were quieting. Under his fingers, the horse was warm and lathered from a fast ride. Brad passed his hand back and traced out the brand. It was one he did not know, and without a light he could not read it.

Moving away from the horse, he stopped in the shade of a big cottonwood that bulked near the veranda of the house. Someone came out of the bunkhouse, his laughter hooting through the night. Brad waited, and when the man had gone again, he eased himself against the wall of the house and up to a window where he could look in.

So Olaf had been right! Brad had a view of the near end of the parlor and resting at ease in a chair was Ike

Quarles. Standing before him, feet spread wide, was Dave Arden. And Arden was arguing like a man who was very sure of himself in Quarles' presence.

Brad could get none of the words, but the gestures Arden made were eloquent enough. He was steamed up about something. Quarles was taking it without any expression.

Brad shifted, trying to find a place where he might be able to hear, but the bunkhouse noises had grown louder, covering all sound. He was engrossed, trying to sift out that sound and catch the talk from inside, and so he did not near the footfalls until a clod rolled under the boot of a man behind him.

Brad spun, his hand slapping for his gun. But he was too late and the bandage around his body made him too slow. Newt was framed in the light coming from the window. There was a smirk of evil satisfaction on his face, and he carried a .44 aimed at Brad's middle.

"Step out, you!"

Brad stepped, his hands held high, though it was an effort to put them there. But there was the barest hope that Olaf might see that cutting out of the light and, in seeing it, understand.

Newt's breath rasped through his loose lips when he saw who it was. "Now won't the boss be interested! The tough drifter!" The gun dipped a little. "Heard you was back. Start walking."

Brad knew only too well what this meant. He had saved Quarles a lot of trouble and explaining. He was trespassing, and Quarles could have him shot and there would be no questions asked. An accident in the dark was explanation enough. No man could openly put much blame on Double Q if that happened.

Newt wiggled the gun again. "Walk," he ordered harshly.

Brad lowered his arms and started moving slowly. He put a whine in his voice, stalling for time. "Maybe we can make a deal, Newt."

"Yeh," Newt answered. "I got a friend who's carrying your bullet. He'd be glad to give it back to you." He laughed at his own humor. "How's that for a deal, Jordan?"

"A little gold don't go bad, Newt," Brad suggested. "A——"

Newt wasn't listening. Both men heard it at the same time. The thunder of hoofs thudding against the night. Olaf was coming in, all right, and making noise enough to raise a graveyard. Brad heard Newt's withdrawn breath, and the man made the mistake of stepping back out of Brad's reach so he could turn and see what was coming. In the frozen instant that Newt's head twisted away, Brad dived at him, slashing at his gun wrist.

Newt pivoted around and his gun crashed, the muzzle flame burning cruelly across Brad's arm. But the gun was down on the ground and Newt was swinging his fists wildly, roaring for help.

Men boiled from the bunkhouse and the front door of Quarles' house slammed. Brad ducked and caught Newt with a short, jarring left that sent the man staggering backward. Olaf came riding wildly on Brad's palomino. The men in the yard scattered as the horse swept through them. Olaf drew rein sharply as Newt's barrel-shaped body staggered in front of his horse and then, with cold deliberation, he sawed on the reins. The horse reared with the unexpected pressure and then plunged down, his front hoofs lunging. Newt flung up one arm, and a wild scream broke from his mouth, keening high in terror.

Brad whispered, "God Almighty!" as Olaf brought the horse up again, driving it onto Newt's threshing body. There was another cry and a dull, snapping sound.

"Ride back!" Brad cried at Olaf, and broke for the cover of the big cottonwood trees. The men in the yard had got their wits about them now and guns flamed.

Olaf did as he was told, digging his heels into the palomino. His big body was loose in the saddle, but he rode bent low, and the darkness swallowed him. Brad stayed where he was for a second and then raced over the soft grass to the strange horse tied near the veranda. He had a glimpse of Quarles standing in the light of the front door, a cigar in one hand. But the noise boiling from the yard seemed to confuse rather than help him.

"What is it?" Quarles bellowed. "Newt! Where are you? Damn it, Newt!"

Untying the reins, Brad slid into the saddle and put the horse for the far corner of the house. "There he goes!" someone yelled, and a shot screamed a foot above Brad's head. He could hear Arden's voice rising in a steady swearing from the veranda.

The men were still milling around as he reached the knoll where he had left Olaf. He found him there, astride the bay again, holding the palomino by the reins. Brad left the strange horse for his own.

"I got your signal," Olaf said quietly.

"What a way to kill a man," Brad said, but without censure.

He understood when Olaf said simply, "He beat us." That would be Olaf's way, gentle until aroused, but possessed then with the terrible wildness of the easy man who is pushed too far.

They stayed where they were in a puddle of darkness. When some of the Double Q men mounted, Brad headed the strange horse down the slope and quirted it. The animal hit the yard running full speed, went through the patch of light too swiftly to be more than glimpsed,

and was gone down the road toward the valley. Brad
watched as the Double Q hands streamed down the
the road after it.

But, should some of them be smarter, he led the way
quickly toward the west hills, staying in shadow as much
as possible and seeking grass to keep the hoofbeats muffled.

"It was Arden," he told Olaf. It had been reckless
going there, he thought. Yet he had found out a good
deal. Arden's waiting and hedging made sense now
where it had not before. And even though it gave
Quarles further reason to ride on him at once, it had
been worth the risk to find this out.

"Arden's been stalling Miss June so she couldn't last
till winter," he explained to Olaf. "That was his game
with Quarles, and now they'll know it's over. So the
waiting is done, Olaf. They'll shoot on sight from here
on in."

"Yah," Olaf agreed calmly. And they rode on without
further comment.

CHAPTER SEVENTEEN

BEFORE Arden could answer Quarles' accusation that
he was getting spooky, the sound of hoofs hammered
loudly in the room. Quarles got up quickly, and both
men started for the door. A gunshot barked close by.
Quarles jerked open the door and plowed onto the
veranda, his cigar still in his fingers. The noise of running men and the fast-moving horse was cut sharply by
an unmistakable scream of pain coming from Newt.
Someone else shouted, and Arden's horse suddenly came
to life and wheeled into the night.

, Arden's swearing rose up. Another gun cracked suddenly. Quarles squinted into the darkness, unable to see more than blurs of shadow. His demanding voice went unheard. Soon the horse came back, moving too fast for anyone to see whether or not it carried a low-bent rider.

Men boiled downhill after the animal. Quarles turned in rage to Arden. "You fool! You were followed."

From the side of the house Newt's voice was crying in pain, the sound growing weaker. Quarles left the veranda, shouting for a lantern. When it was brought, he looked down at Newt. The foreman was twisted in the dirt as if he had been tied in a knot and flung to the ground. Great beads of sweat coursed down his streaked face and blood and foam bubbled from his mouth.

"Jordan," he gasped. "Tricked me. The Swede ran me down with a horse."

Quarles put his hands out, and Newt screamed again as fingers probed at him. Quarles stood up, his face ugly in the lantern light. "Back's broke." He watched the blood coming from Newt's mouth. "Busted inside, too."

While they watched, Newt's gasp rose up and then faded out. After a moment he lay still. Quarles turned slowly away. "He's done," he said grimly. "Take care of him." He started for the house.

Back on the veranda he waited for Arden. "If Jordan gets away, the news of you being here will spread all over the valley."

Arden took a deep breath and steadied his trembling hands until he could shape a cigarette. "If it does," he answered, "I'll say I was trying to deal with you on the water. I'll go to June now and give her the story. That'll stop Jordan."

"If it's believed," Quarles said skeptically. His was a

suspicious mind, and he could not understand anyone who would not have the same kind of reasoning.

"Even if it isn't, it'll still give us time," Arden argued.

"I'm not ready. Not until Parker's out of the way," Quarles said.

"There's no help for it," Arden objected. "Get rid of Parker and we can start."

Quarles seemed to be considering it. "Leave any messages with Keinlan," he ordered. "I've got to think on it." He threw the stub of his dead cigar into the yard. "Now get home and mend your fences."

Arden went to borrow a Double Q mount, and Quarles stood on the veranda until all sound of the man and horse had faded out. Then he went to the corral and ordered his own horse. He was no longer dull with anger; he moved with the cold steadiness of a man whose mind is made up. As he followed the trail Arden had taken, he said aloud:

"Newt was worth a dozen of that fool."

Halfway to town he met his men riding back. He lit a match and held it up to identify himself. The group was leading a riderless horse.

"Got away," one of them said.

Quarles' voice was flat and empty. "Shoot Jordan or the Swede on sight." Dropping the match, he rode on toward town.

Putting his horse behind the Sawhorse Saloon, he went to the upstairs room and sent for Keinlan. When he came, Quarles laid out his orders bluntly.

"I want to know what's really bothering Arden." He told Keinlan of the night's trouble and of Arden's edginess. "Arden will be in looking for me soon. See that you find out then."

"I'll try," Keinlan said indifferently. But when Quarles

had gone down to the poker tables, Keinlan's eyes were thoughtful and there was the faintest of smiles on his drooping mouth.

Since he was in town, Quarles decided to sit in on a game. He prided himself on being able to turn events to his own advantage before another man got hold of them. He was satisfied with the plan he had formed, and his spirits rose as he won three straight pots in the game.

He left then, on impulse, and hurried his horse until he could see Biddle's place. There was still a light, and he turned toward it. He got to Biddle as he was ready for bed. Quarles told him quickly what had happened.

"Arden wants to move in on you," Quarles pointed out.

Biddle rubbed a hand worriedly across his mouth. "I put no brand on that stock, Ike. I done just what you said. We got two hundred head boxed in now, but I ain't branded it."

"If you do," Quarles told him, "see that Arden's brand gets slapped on." He laughed harshly. "He's put it on his horses already, figuring it's about time for the A-in-a-D to be on the range." He made a show of leaving, and then turned casually.

"I'd see to Arden pretty soon, Nick. He's getting so he don't like you here."

Comprehension began to work into Biddle's scooped features. He lifted his lamp and started for the bedroom. "I'll see to him," he said.

"But not until I say so," Quarles warned.

"I can wait," Biddle said.

Brad rode into the Split S yard and went quietly to the old barn. Getting the two packs he had put together, he slipped out as silently as he had come. He had not planned on using them so soon, but now he was glad they were ready for him. He and Olaf camped high on the Split S range at the edge of the timber. Before the first daylight they were up, and long before the sun rose Brad was across on Biddle's land, looking for tracks leading from the place where the Split S fence had been torn out and repaired.

It was still early when he found the grass-bottomed draw that held a herd of Split S beef. He guessed somewhere around three hundred head was in here. There was no guard; this fine grass and a spring close by kept the stock content.

"Biddle did this," Brad said, "and Arden didn't seem to like it."

"Do we take them back?" Olaf questioned.

"Back to Split S," Brad agreed, "but not to the same place." Noticing Olaf's puzzled expression, he said, "Olaf, when you start hitting a man, keep on hitting until you're done with him. When you get him in a corner, keep him there. Being soft is fine for some people, but Quarles isn't soft, and you can't fight him that way."

He rolled a cigarette, and when he looked over it at Olaf his eyes were bleak. "We hit Quarles twice now. We got to keep on hitting him or he'll get out of the corner. He's got more power than we have. Remember that. Hit and keep hitting."

"Yah," Olaf agreed gravely. And Brad could see that he was remembering the beating at the homestead.

"So," Brad went on, "we take this stock into Pine Canyon. I got an idea. If it works we've got Quarles closer to where we want him." He shook his head as if to clear it of heaviness. "Quarles won't wait and Arden won't wait. I'm not waiting from here on."

He thought of Arden with bitterness. Faith McFee was

promised to him and June Grant trusted in him. There
was nothing that Brad could do yet. Not to Arden. How
could he make the others understand? He was a newcomer, a man they thought of as brutal—a drifter; his
word would be worth nothing. He would have to wait
for a way to show the real Arden to Faith and June
Grant. With a motion of anger he started for the herd
of beef.

Olaf worked willingly and, after a few instructions,
did his share in getting the stock moving. Brad led them
out of the draw and over a little rise that led to Split S
graze. From here he angled toward Pine Canyon. It was
slow going and a few head escaped Olaf's efforts back
at drag, but the distance wasn't far, and before the sun
was straight overhead the first of the beef was going
between the two tall pines that marked the mouth of
the canyon.

Brad moved aside and let them go. The telltale sign
of smoke coming from the line shack inside warned him
that there were still Sawhorse or Double Q men here.

Half the cattle were in when Brad heard a rider coming from up canyon. He and Olaf sat around a pointed
ledge, out of sight of the canyon mouth. The rider appeared, moving easily in and out of the drifting cattle.
He was a man Brad had never seen before and, telling
Olaf to stay out of sight, Brad rode into view.

"Where you been?" he demanded. "Biddle said you'd
help move this bunch." He scowled at the man, who was
slack-jawed with surprise. "I only get paid to do one
man's work."

"Who in hell are you?" the man asked.

Brad gave a name offhand and repeated his question.
The hand had evidently been up here too long to have
heard of his return. This was what Brad had hoped for.
If it had turned out otherwise, his gun was ready to

take over the argument. Now the man shook his head.

"I got no orders," he said.

"You're getting them," Brad told him. "Biddle said he was sending someone to tell you. You're supposed to move the other stock out to where this came from."

The man's eyes, set deep in a thin face, flickered with suspicion. "Since when?"

"Since last night," Brad said flatly. "Split S hired a crew of hardcases and they're getting proddy. Biddle wants this stuff where it won't be found." A smile twisted the corner of his mouth. "And if it is found, who's to say this canyon ain't Split S graze anyway?" He laughed at the joke. The other man smiled faintly, and then guffawed as he caught on to the idea.

"Nick didn't figure that one out," he said.

"No, Quarles did."

The man seemed satisfied. He swung his horse. "All right, help me move the other out."

"I got some strays to pick up," Brad told him. "You ain't crippled."

The man shrugged and rode back into the canyon, hoorawing the tag end of the stock as he went. Brad chuckled softly on his way back to Olaf. He explained his plan carefully to the big man, and when he had finished Olaf nodded, a broad smile of anticipation on his face.

Brad left his horse and climbed, following a faint deer trail until he could look down into Pine Canyon. He could see three men working below, shunting the Split S stock off to one side and rounding up the Double Q and Sawhorse beef. They had not put too much on, Brad observed, just enough to stake a claim to the grass. It was a weak enough claim, but with three men to hold it, June Grant had been able to do little.

In a short while eighty-odd head of beef started for

the mouth of the canyon and Brad eased back to the level. He staked himself at one side of the mouth, leaving Olaf on the other. The thin-faced man he had talked to came out presently, riding point, and Brad showed himself to view. His gun was held loosely in his hand.

"Friend," he said softly, "just ride to your right."

The man gaped at him and looked as if he might go for his gun. Brad lifted his own, making his point plain. With his hands held away from his sides, the man moved to the right. Suddenly a large arm snaked out, catching him by the throat. He made a single squawking sound and disappeared.

Brad slipped back out of sight. The beef began to pour through. This was the ticklish time, with two men to handle. They came, finally, out of the thin dust the cattle were throwing up. Brad knew neither man. Once more he rode into sight.

"Lift 'em," he ordered brusquely.

One man did as he was told, but the other reached for his gun. Brad sent a shot snapping at his hat and his hands went up hurriedly. Loyalty, Brad knew, went as far as a man's pay in cases like this, and he had counted on the fact that these two would figure they weren't being paid to buck odds.

Olaf rode out at Brad's call and with surprising deftness roped both men. He went away and came back, leading the first man also roped to his horse. "Now," Brad said, "we'll take a little trip."

They went sullenly, unable to do more than guide their horses the way he directed. Carefully, Brad made a wide swing so that he came down at the town from the west. After a short distance the mountains leveled into sage hills and then dropped lower until they were on the flats. Coming in from this direction they met no one.

It took a little time to find a way across the river gully, but finally Brad herded his captives to town, coming in from below the One-Shot Saloon. Here he stopped and had Olaf remove the ropes.

"Just keep on like I say," he warned. "If you don't think we can shoot, try running."

They continued their sullen riding right up to the front of the jail. The blacksmith's boy, Jube, was on the street, and his mouth fell open at the sight of the drifter and the big Swede herding two Sawhorse men and a Double Q rider into the jail.

McFee was at his desk, his feet cocked up. They came down with a thump when Brad pushed the men in. Brad said, "Found these three, Sheriff. Wearing guns in town. Figure you'd want to know."

"He prodded us into town!" the thin-faced man blustered.

Brad took his gun and laid it on a chair, near to hand, and motioned to Olaf to do the same. "Ours are checked," he said. The cold humor glinted in his eyes. "But these are plain lawbreakers, McFee. I say lock 'em up."

The thin-faced man squawked again. McFee growled at them. He looked angry, and Brad realized it was directed at him. "Sawhorse and Double Q," he muttered.

"Break laws like everyone else," Brad said. His eyes met those of the sheriff and held steadily. "You ever been to Pine Canyon, Sheriff? Pretty place." He went on softly. "And full of Split S beef. I counted three hundred head. And Split S fence was knocked down yesterday."

"I'm not the law in the valley," the sheriff said stiffly.

"These men are in town wearing guns. Are you the law here?"

McFee pressed his lips tightly together. This was a pretty obvious box Jordan had squeezed him into. He hesitated, weighing the outcome of this. His anger at Brad tipped the scales.

Brad thought he understood what was eating at Mc-Fee, but he didn't let up. The humor was gone from him now, leaving his eyes a flinty gray. He continued to stare at the sheriff until McFee lowered his own gaze.

"I can't hold them," he said. "They got a chance to check their guns. If not, then they'll have to ride out."

The thin-faced man protested, "And let him trail us and do it all over again?"

"I'm not the law in the valley," McFee answered. "He can do what he wants out of town."

Brad had half expected this, yet it sickened him. He jerked his head. "Go on and ride," he said. "Go tell Biddle and Quarles." His voice sharpened. "But the next time you touch Split S beef or put your foot in Pine Canyon I start shooting."

The thin-faced man started to laugh, saw Brad's face, and swallowed back the sound. He led the others out; they mounted and rode hard going north. Brad turned from the doorway to the sheriff.

"Thanks for the help, McFee."

"I ain't the law in the valley and——"

"The valley's bigger than the town," Brad said. "When Quarles has swallowed everything there, this place won't be a good bite. Remember that."

McFee sat down, trembling. "Get the hell out of my office!" he ordered.

CHAPTER EIGHTEEN

IN THE MORNING Arden took the team and spring wagon and headed for town. He had seen no sign of Jordan, nor heard any repercussions of the night before. Quarles' men might have caught Jordan and Hegstrom, he thought, but his hopes were not high. Jordan was too clever a man to be easily trapped.

The worry over what had happened and what could come of it lay heavy on his mind. That, coupled with the rustling of the Split S beef by Biddle, ate into him steadily as he rode along. When he paused and looked across at Quarles' and Biddle's fields he felt no better. They were done with haymaking there. The great stacks stood solid and rich, waiting for winter.

Close around him was the yellow Split S hay, and the sight of it put a bitter taste in his mouth. He was all too aware of the position Quarles had placed him in. Should Quarles decide to throw against him, Arden knew he would be squeezed out with no recourse. Even if June went under and he got his opportunity to take over, without hay he would be no better off than she. If Quarles chose not to let him have winterfeed, where was he?

The idea of it grew stronger, nourished by Quarles' attitude of last night. By the time Arden reached town he had worked himself into a mood of sullen revengefulness. Leaving the team behind the Sawhorse Saloon, he went first to the store and got his machinery, and after that stopped briefly to speak to Faith. Then he walked deliberately up the stairs to Keinlan's office. He went in without knocking.

He was ready for a showdown talk with Quarles, and when he found only Keinlan in the office it took him a moment to adjust to the situation. Keinlan regarded him in silence, studying Arden's dark scowl.

"Something eating you?" Keinlan asked pleasantly.

"I want to see Quarles."

"Not here yet," Keinlan said. He measured his man

and decided that this was the time. "Have a drink," he said without joviality.

Arden's suspicion showed. "Since when you getting so friendly?" he demanded in a surly tone.

Keinlan took one of his cigars and rustled it between his long fingers. "You come in here looking for Quarles and on the prod," he answered. His drooping eyelids shut out anything Arden might want to see. "That makes you what some would call a kindred spirit."

The suspicion stayed openly on Arden's face. He had never liked this man because he had never really known him. Keinlan was just a flickering character who moved in and out of his saloon; Arden had never been able to pin him down. He only knew that when a man was down and out Keinlan usually had a hand in helping him. But outside of that he had no clues to the mind of the saloon owner.

Now Arden said, "My business with Quarles is private."

"Sure," Keinlan agreed easily. "Nobody knows about it but you and him and me." He paused and added dryly, "And most of the Double Q hands."

Arden's baffled anger started to twist toward this man who was obviously goading him. And then he stopped it. Thoughtfully, he took a chair and shaped a cigarette. Keinlan wasn't talking just to hear his own words, Arden suspected. There was meaning here if he could get at it.

"Say what you're trying to," he ordered. Touching a match to his cigarette, he sucked smoke in deeply. His eyes watched Keinlan over the top of the flame, but there was nothing in that long drooping face to give him a hint of what went on behind it.

"Quarles is starting to move," Keinlan said. He laid down his unlit cigar and pressed the tips of his fingers together. "He's got it figured to get rid of the ones in his way before he goes up against the Split S."

"Split S is nothing," Arden said curtly.

"Not even with Jordan there now?" Keinlan countered. He saw Arden's surprised expression. "Sure," he went on, "what's between you and Quarles is your private business. Only Quarles was in last night telling me what happened."

"Why?" Arden demanded. He was no longer making much effort to hide his feelings from Keinlan. His wonder over all this was plain.

"Quarles thinks you're up to something," Keinlan said blandly. "He wants me to find out what it is."

Arden took a deep drag from his cigarette; his hand shook noticeably. "Why?" he demanded again.

"I told you, Quarles figured on getting rid of the ones in his way," Keinlan answered. His half-shut eyes flickered. He was a patient man; he had waited a long time for what was soon to come.

"But I'm with him," Arden cried. "I'm not against him." He got to his feet, his anger forgotten in a rush of fear. In that moment he could see what he had schemed for being drawn away from him, inch by tantalizing inch. "Him and me——"

Keinlan's voice was smooth. "He don't trust you, Arden. You're smart, maybe too smart for him. He's afraid of that."

The smooth talk went over Arden, easing his fright and giving him a chance to think again. Once more his suspicion returned, directed at Keinlan. "You're his man. Why tell me this?"

"I'm my own man," Keinlan said. "Quarles thinks I'm his man. He thinks you are, too."

Arden sat down again, his breathing heavy. "You haven't said anything yet."

"Quarles wants Split S," Keinlan told him. "He and Biddle figure on having everything worth having on the west side, including your two-bit piece. When that's swallowed, they'll be too big to hold and they'll go east."

"I was to get Split S," Arden said furiously. "That was in the deal."

"So it was," Keinlan murmured, and his smile made a point of it.

Arden flung his cigarette angrily toward a spittoon and immediately began to roll another. He sat hunched over, smoking fitfully, turning Keinlan's words over, letting them work into his mind. The more he thought about them, the more sense they made. Particularly after last night.

He straightened up and dropped the second cigarette after the first one. "Bring out that drink," he said.

Keinlan was careful, apparently matching Arden drink for drink. But he knew his own capacity, and he knew how to make another man think he was taking on as big a load or bigger. He did little talking until the contents of the bottle were well along toward the bottom.

Arden's breathing had become heavy. His thirst, fed by injured anger, was consuming him. He was not a heavy drinking man except when pressures grew too great for him. Usually he was too much aware of his weakness toward liquor, and he stayed carefully away from more than one or two Saturday night glasses.

Keinlan saw the liquor sweat on Arden's forehead and he moved in, still cautiously. "Quarles figures on getting you in a tight place and then you'll have to work for him and get nothing for it."

Arden wiped at his forehead. "I've got more savvy than Quarles. Let him think it. When the squeeze comes, he'll get caught, not me."

"That's right," Keinlan said. "You play it right and that's the way it'll be." He lifted the bottle and poured Arden a shot with exaggerated care.

Arden drank and mulled it over. He drank again, and finally he burst out, "So he thinks he'll get me before I get him!"

"He counts on it." Keinlan was willing to wait, to play this along until it came out of Arden of his own free will. It was not long. Arden began to see Keinlan in a new light. Here was a man he had misjudged. Here was a friend when one was needed. Keinlan would help him outwit Quarles. And help him get rid of this new threat to his plans—Jordan. Keinlan could see Arden's ideas forming, and he dropped just enough of the right words to make them come.

"Jordan's dangerous, too," Arden said. "Maybe it was just luck that he happened to go to Quarles' last night, and maybe he figured it out. I don't know."

"That doesn't matter," Keinlan said. "What does matter is the fact that he went and saw you there."

"I can straighten it out with June Grant," Arden said. "But it don't make things any easier."

"Not for you, maybe," Keinlan said. "But it makes things easier for Quarles."

Something in the tone of his voice brought Arden's head up with a jerk. He focused his eyes carefully on the saloon owner. "What do you mean?"

"See what Quarles would do?" Keinlan asked. "Now he can have Jordan killed and you blamed for it. If anybody was to question it, he could point out that Jordan was accusing you of trying to hurt the Split S. Or maybe he'll have you killed and Jordan blamed. He could give the same reasons. One way or the other, you'd be done, Arden."

"He won't get a chance," Arden said hotly. "Damn him!"

"That's right," Keinlan agreed. "We'll get him." He made a deliberate hiccoughing sound. "You and me."

Suspicion came back to Arden. "What you getting out of it?"

"My half," Keinlan said. "You take the upper end of the valley. "I'll take this end and the town. And plenty of water."

Arden thought it over. He reached for the whisky bottle. "A deal!" he said. He poured himself a drink and downed it. Keinlan waited for it to hit him, and when it did Keinlan caught him as he fell forward, soddenly asleep, and dragged him to the couch.

Smiling, Keinlan went downstairs to wait for Quarles.

Together Brad and Olaf went into the restaurant after leaving the sheriff's office. It was between dinner and supper, but seeing it open reminded Brad that he had had no meal since breakfast. "Eat while we can now," he advised Olaf. "We may get caught short for time."

Olaf was only too willing to eat, and they took places at the counter. Faith served them, but with none of the friendliness she had shown the day before. Brad wore his gun openly and he saw that she was looking at it.

"There's no teeth in the sheriff's law any more," he said flatly.

Her coolness crystallized into open contempt. "So now you're strong enough to flout an old man, too," she said. Her voice sharpened. "I was in back of the office just a little while ago and heard what you tried to do." The contempt roughened, riding over him. "You can't be satisfied with causing June Grant trouble before she's ready; you try to cause it in town, too."

Brad studied her for a quiet moment. Her eyes met his and she did not look away. Whatever this was that had a grip on her, he saw that she believed in it completely.

"Arden's been talking to you," he said in a tone of sudden understanding.

Faith tossed her head. "He has. This morning."

"Ah," Brad said, "that's your mistake, then."

"Mistake?" she cried. "Is it a mistake to know that you're trying to use Dave and June to settle your grudge against Quarles? And trying to use my uncle for the same purpose?"

Brad could not fathom this girl. It seemed that there was no pleasing her. And yet, in a way, he could not put the blame on her. Arden was a smooth man with his tongue, and he had been shrewd enough to turn to his own advantage the fact that he had been caught at Quarles' place. Brad had liked Faith McFee since their first meeting, and it dug into him to see her taken in by Arden.

"When I came here," he said to her now, "I had no fight with Quarles. I have reason enough now, but it was through you and your uncle I got into this. June Grant asked for help, and we're trying to give it to her." He met her gaze with cold anger showing in his eyes. "Do you think we came back just for Ike Quarles? I could ride in and shoot him and go if that was all."

As he looked at her, her eyes faltered and slid away. She was an honest person with herself as a rule and she could not deny that these things he said were true. Yet she had to put her trust in something—and Arden had said otherwise.

"Dave told me——" she began.

Brad got up and laid a coin on the counter, his lips

clamped tight to hold back the scathing words waiting there. At the door he turned. "If the sheriff wants to press his law, I'll be at the One-Shot."

She picked up the plates. "Do your own taunting," she said coldly. When the door had slammed she walked away, dropping the plates in a deep pan. She stood with her hands in the soapy water, feeling the throb of anger slowly diminishing at her temples.

"Brutal," she whispered. But was his way the wrong way? Without consciously trying, she found herself making a comparison between Brad and Dave Arden. The result brought a flush to her checks, and with a sudden tightening of her full mouth she tore her mind from the subject. An idea came, lingering until she was forced to recognize it. She would have to talk to Dave again. This morning he had been hurried and quick. Perhaps there was more than she had sensed in his words.

CHAPTER NINETEEN

On the short ride to the One-Shot, Brad studied the town and found it quiet. Those few people on the street were marked in their disinterest toward him and Olaf. It would have amused him before, but now he realized that in this neutrality there was meaning. His return was understood as a challenge to Quarles, and there were none who dared side openly with one or the other.

"They'll wait until they can smell the wind," he said to Olaf, "and then they'll run to get behind it."

He did not see Keinlan, who had watched him from the time he had first come until now. If he had, it would not have worried him; he knew nothing of the man.

It was Doc Stebbins Brad sought, and he located him

in his office at the rear of the saloon. He was finishing a sleep and there was puffiness on his usually cheerful face. But there was none of the friendliness that Brad had expected.

"Professional visit or otherwise?" the Doc asked.

"You wanted to see me," Brad reminded him.

"You took long enough," Doc Stebbins answered. He shook himself like a dog coming out of water. "You took too long."

Brad dropped to the edge of an ancient sofa and shaped a cigarette. "So," he said when it was finished, "there's no help here, either."

"You're rushing things," the Doc said irritably.

He had heard, too, Brad realized. He said, "Five weeks —six? However many I've been here." His voice was level. "Split S hay is dried out. Split S beef has been rustled. I found three hundred prime steers today. I'm hurrying things."

"Split S isn't ready to fight," the Doc objected. "What have you got? June's three hands are useless. That leaves Arden and you two. What is that against Quarles?"

Brad was weary of hearing this refrain, of seeing the way these people were acting. He would have given his help had they not asked for it. The fact that they did ask made him think they should give some in return. But one hint that it was time to move and they all crawled toward their holes. Too often he had seen apathy or fear let a man like Quarles get a grip on a whole county.

"Arden was with Quarles last night," Brad said. This was a thing he had not intended to tell, but since Arden had already said it himself, he saw no reason to keep quiet any longer.

"Faith told me," the Doc said. "Arden spoke to her this morning. He was trying to deal with Quarles. He was close to getting somewhere before you busted it up."

"That's the way of it," Brad agreed, but his smile was bitter and caustic. "Did he also say he had been to Quarles more than the once? Olaf saw him riding there this spring."

Doc Stebbins rubbed his hand over a bristly chin. "That could mean a number of things," he said thoughtfully.

Brad realized impatiently that the Doc was not even going to try to understand. He stood up. "I'll get no help here, I see."

"Not until June is ready," Doc Stebbins said. "We can't risk turning Quarles on her yet. If it's not already too late," he added heavily.

"You won't help, but you'll hinder me," Brad said.

"Which is saying we'll help Quarles," the Doc rejoined heatedly. His face was beginning to redden wtih anger. "We'll not do that, either."

"Then," Brad asked, "why is Quarles trying to get Parker out of here?" If he could get nothing else, he might get those last bits of information he had not yet gathered.

"He's smart. And," Doc Stebbins said, "before Parker came, Quarles was courting June Grant." Even in anger there was a quick note in his voice. "Or courting her grassland. She wasn't encouraging him but, even so, he got the idea that Parker was at fault. It hurt his pride."

Brad could understand more about Ike Quarles now. "His pride is that deep, then?"

"That deep," the Doc agreed.

Brad went to the door. "One more thing and then you can go back to your sleeping. Where does Quarles come when he's in town?"

"The Sawhorse," Doc Stebbins answered. As the door opened he added, "So now you—"

"Think what you like," Brad retorted, and left. With Olaf following in silence, he rode to the Sawhorse, tied in front, and went inside.

It was a dim place, musty with the smell of stale beer and of men who worked more than they washed. Ike Quarles was standing at the bar, drinking beer and talking to a thin man Brad did not know. The few loafers in the room silenced their talk, and Quarles turned to see who had come in.

Brad's voice was quiet but loud enough to carry. "I moved your beef out of Pine Canyon today," he told Quarles. "I put Split S stock in."

Quarles stood very still. The fingers wrapped around his beer glass grew white with his effort at control. The tall man beside him moved quietly aside and went around behind the bar.

"And I'm going up to homestead that meadow now," Brad went on. His tone was flat but the taunt in his words was obvious.

Quarles' breathing was heavy. His big, flabby body stirred as he moved a step forward. Then he stepped back and stood still again. "You can come here with a gun and talk like that," he said.

"Wear yours next time," Brad answered. "MeFee won't stop you." He turned, pushing open the batwing doors, and stepped to the board walk. Anger was still prodding him. He knew the feeling and he knew, too, the danger in the recklessness such anger always brought. At the moment his indignation was no greater with Quarles than with the people of the town.

As they rode back toward the Split S, however, he began to work it over in his mind. In a measure he could understand the townspeople. He could not agree with them, and his contempt was not lessened even though he saw their position plainly enough. Had he been a man of less determination, he would have given up the desire that brought him here and ridden on. But no matter how McFee acted, no matter how any of them acted, he had promised to help June Grant, and he intended to finish what he had started. He had never been a man to turn off a trail once he had begun to follow it.

It was for that reason he had first decided to go through with the homesteading plan. Since talking with Faith and the Doc he had found other, more immediate reasons. He had offered a challenge openly to Quarles. If it did not draw the man out, the town and the valley would know soon enough, and Quarles would be the one to walk softly.

Quarles would know this, too, Brad realized, and there would be little waiting now before the Double Q was ordered to hit him.

At the Split S, Brad found no one but June Grant. He spoke plainly, as he had the day before. "This morning we moved your beef into Pine Canyon," he told her. "There were three hundred head at Biddle's."

She seemed bewildered and uncertain, and Brad knew that Arden had got to her, too. "You're afraid that Quarles will come," he said.

"I'm sick of waiting," she said. "But—"

"But," he finished for her, "you have to trust me or Arden. It can't be both any more."

"I've known Dave for two years," she said. There was pleading in her voice, and indecision as well.

"And me for maybe a month," he said. "We'll ride now."

She put out a hand. "Please. I don't know what to do."

"I do," Brad said. "I'm going to homestead that meadow where Quarles has his water. I already told him, so he'll waste himself on me instead of coming here."

"You're doing it to keep him away from here?"

"Partly," Brad answered. "The rest is for myself. I want the land."

She looked at him as if only the last part of what he had said registered with her. "Oh."

Brad went out and hitched the team to the wagon, tying their saddle horses behind. He and Olaf were starting down the road when June Grant came out. He said, "I'd be obliged if you'd tell Parker I'd like to see him."

"I will," she said. The indecision was still with her.

"If," he added, "we're all still alive." Tipping his hat, he started the team again.

It was growing late when he finally got them through the forest and up to Olaf's old cabin. He saw that Newt had been shrewd enough to leave it standing to give the impression Brad and Olaf had ridden out. The pack horse had been taken, Brad supposed, to Double Q or had been destroyed. At the moment it made no difference; there were other things to be concerned with.

Getting down, Brad went inside and found the cabin completely empty. It was as he had expected. They had cleaned out everything. He took a lantern from the supplies in the wagon, and with its light walked to where he had first started shooting at Newt. He found what he sought nearly buried in forest duff. It was his bone-handled .44, and the familiar weight on his leg was a good feeling.

"We'll drive this stuff as close to the meadow as we can," he told Olaf, "and pack it in the rest of the way."

There was still a little light when they left the trees, but it was all used up long before they had finished the job. They had to leave the wagon a good quarter of a mile from the meadow and, using the team as pack horses, move their goods in that way. With the last of the daylight Brad found a ledge on the east wall enclosing the meadow, and he chose this place for a camp. It was not too good but a shallow overhang offered some protection and it was up out of the soggy bottom.

He arranged their supplies in front of the overhang in the manner of a low wall. The guns and ammunition he put where they could be reached easily. Olaf cut firewood while he finished the task, and then they ate a quick meal. Brad had put out the fire as soon as the meal was cooked and they sat in the dark, listening to the water sounds from the meadow below.

"You get some sleep," he told Olaf. "We'll take turns watching."

"Yah," Olaf said stolidly, and crawled into his blankets at the back of the overhang.

This waiting was a thing Brad did not like, yet he saw no way around it. Without a force of men he could do no good attacking the Double Q and that, without open provocation, was not his way had he the men. He could only draw Quarles out and strike and draw him out again. Sooner or later, he knew, Quarles would grow too weak to fight—or he would win quickly by the sheer weight of numbers.

CHAPTER TWENTY

Dave Arden awoke with a raging thirst. It took him a little while to realize where he was, and longer to stand on his feet without dizziness overcoming him. He wanted to lie down again, to soak up more sleep, but the thirst was too strong, and he started down the stairs for the bar.

He had nearly reached the bottom when he heard Brad Jordan's level, cold voice and Quarles' reply. Arden stopped, drawing back so he would not be seen, and listened. He was still there after Jordan left. He wanted that drink, but he had no desire to run into Quarles. Not right now.

Cursing under his breath, he dragged himself back up the stairs and down the hall. Finally he reached the outside. With an effort he slicked up at the horse pump in the yard and made his way across the street to the restaurant. It was late for suppertime and there were only two men waiting for their meal. With a surly grunt to them, he took his usual seat at the far end of the counter.

Faith came over to him as soon as she had waited on the two men. "Give me some water," Arden said hoarsely.

Silently she brought him a glass of water. After a moment's study of him, she went away and returned with a full pitcher. She set it in front of him.

"That's not necessary!" he said resentfully. He gulped the glass of water and started to pour another. She could not help noticing that his hand shook until the mouth of the pitcher chattered against the edge of the glass.

"It was my joke," she said, still quietly. "I'm sorry."

He looked up, caught her expression, and lowered his eyes again. There was nothing in him but fire from the liquor. He was a fool for having come in here.

"Go in the back room and lie down," she suggested.

"I'm all right. Let me alone," he said in a low, angry voice.

"I've never seen you like this before," she remarked wonderingly.

"It doesn't happen often," he retorted. "Let me alone, can't you?"

Her patience stretched thin and snapped. "Yes," she answered shortly, "I can." She walked away to serve some other men who had come in, leaving Arden to brood

before the pitcher of water. He tried to work up a cigarette, but his fingers trembled too much, and he threw
the paper savagely to the floor. Without speaking, Faith
brought him a meal and went away again.

He ate it because there was nothing else to do unless
he left the restaurant, and he lacked the energy for that.
But after it was down he felt better; the fire inside him
began to go, and with a second cup of coffee he managed
to roll a cigarette. He was still there, smoking moodily,
when the last of the men cleared out, leaving them alone.

"I'm sorry," he said. She merely looked coldly at him,
and he forced the warm smile to his lips. "Faith, I——" Be
humble, he thought. Be humble as hell. It had worked
before, more times than he could count. He depended
on it to work again.

"A man is always one way or another," she said at
last. "I'll have to get used to that." She brought him
another cup of coffee. He touched her hand gently, but
she did not smile as she usually did when he touched
her. Still, she was no longer cold.

She began to ready the dishes for washing. "Brad Jordan was in today," she said. She told him about it.

"Our beef back in Pine Canyon," Arden muttered.
His head still felt thick; it was hard to force himself to
think. "He'll draw fire sure!"

"That's what he wants, isn't it?" Faith asked.

"It's too soon," he protested.

"So we all told him," she answered. She busied herself with the dishes. So they had, but she was beginning
to wonder. At least Brad Jordan had done something.
While Dave was getting drunk. She tried to put the
thought aside. Her loyalties were strong and it upset her
to think so of Dave Arden. But her honesty was stronger,
and she faced him now.

"What do you plan to do, Dave?"

"Wait," he said. "Quarles will make a mistake and then——"

"Wait? What if he doesn't make a mistake?"

"He will," Arden said briefly.

"Maybe that's what Jordan wants," Faith said carefully, "to force Quarles into a mistake."

"If that's what you think," he began stiffly, then clamped his lips shut. "Jordan will get himself killed and the Split S burned out," he said. "What good is that?"

"What good is waiting?" she asked herself, but she did not let him hear.

Their talk ceased and, after a while, he became aware that the silence was strained. "I'd better get back," he suggested.

"It's about time," she agreed, and went on with her work.

Arden went out into darkness. Across the way he noticed the horses tied there and Quarles' usual big black was not among them. Going around to the rear he saw only his own team and spring wagon. Sure that Quarles was gone, he went inside and up to Keinlan's office. He found Keinlan having a late drink and a cigar.

"You all right?" Keinlan asked.

Arden was startled and a little pleased at this, the first solicitude he had received. "All right," he said.

"You took on quite a load," Keinlan said conversationally.

Arden remembered it vaguely. As he waited, more and more of the day began to come back to him. "I said plenty, too," he blurted out.

"You did."

So he had told Keinlan his idea to outsmart Quarles. Until now he had not been sure. "What will you do?" he asked hesitantly.

"Nothing," Keinlan answered. He looked pained. "We made a partnership deal, didn't we?" His eyes were shrewd on Arden. He had been waiting for his return, and had sent a man to watch the spring wagon. If Arden hadn't come in, he would have sent for him. There was something to be done soon, and he planned on Arden's doing it.

"Quarles was in," Keinlan told him. His smile was unpleasant. "He'll take care of Jordan for you."

"And make it so it looks like I did it?"

Keinlan smiled. "You can beat him to that draw." He saw the interest he had waited for, and he said, "By getting Parker."

Arden shook his head, his disappointment plain. "Quarles won't fool with Parker now for a while. He wants Jordan."

"So he does, and everyone knows it. But if you were to get Parker and make it look like Quarles rode against him, and then get Jordan, too——" He left it unfinished. Left it for Arden's mind to shape.

"I could get Jordan and they'd think he did it," Arden said slowly, softly. Nodding, more to himself than Keinlan, he got up and walked out.

Arden drove home slowly. Whatever Keinlan's idea was, he had no feeling for it tonight. He was still sick from liquor. There was time enough ahead. If Quarles got Jordan tonight that would make it so much the better. If not, he could wait for his own chance.

By morning he felt like himself again, and he worked on the hay machinery steadily. The way he saw it now, Quarles was about forced into moving. It was still too soon, but if Quarles did make his play and take over Split S, then Arden wanted the land in good shape for himself.

June Grant was nervous all day, he noticed. She sent Andy to town about dinnertime on a pretext of getting some flour. Andy Toll was the ranch gossip, and this way she would get what news there was about Jordan.

But at the early supper Andy had nothing to tell her. There was no news from town except that some people seemed worried. McFee was edgy, he told them. Everyone had the idea Jordan was causing a lot of trouble.

After supper Arden saddled his horse and rode to town to mend his fences with Faith. He was slow and careful with her, and when he left to go to the One-Shot for a drink to ease his way home, he thought he had made some progress. He stayed awhile at the One-Shot, watching Jim Parker playing a game of poker. Parker appeared as unconcerned as ever, and that brought to Arden's mind Keinlan's idea. While he sipped his beer he mulled it over.

He was still thinking about it when a shout went up from outside. Jube, the blacksmith's boy, pushed his head in through the batwing doors. "Water!" he bawled. "The river's runnin' with water!"

CHAPTER TWENTY-ONE

OLAF WAKENED BRAD at the first sign of daylight. "Nobody's come," he said. And lay down to catch a nap while Brad built a cautious fire and fixed breakfast.

They were at work early. During the night Brad had crystallized a plan in his mind. He had come here partly to take up this land and partly to draw Quarles' force from the Split S. But Quarles seemed a hard man to drew out, if his silence of the night before was any indication. Brad saw that he would have to hit Quarles harder than he had been hit before, and around this he shaped his plan.

From the supplies they had brought in the wagon, Brad now got the blasting powder and fuse. He set two small charges—one in the cut where the meadow drained out, and one at the lower end where the trail came in. Leaving the powder with waiting fuses, he and Olaf set to work cutting a new ditch.

Brad wiped the sweat off his face after grueling hours of pushing a shovel into the mucky sod and lifting up the dirt. "We don't have to go deep," he pointed out to Olaf. "If we can trap the water in here by plugging the two outlets, the natural slope will help us."

Yah," Olaf answered uncomprehendingly.

Brad pushed his shovel into the dirt. "Let's eat dinner," he said.

While they ate a cold meal, he explained his idea to Olaf. "We can work the water out through this side into the old dry creek bed that goes through your land. My guess is that the water ran down it and back into the Sawhorse before Quarles ditched the meadow." His smile was tight. "All we'll do is put things back the way they were."

Through the long afternoon he felt the pressure mounting. Double Q men should have showed before now, if only to answer the challenge he had flung at Quarles the day before. But there was nothing—no sound but the noise of their own work and the soft gurgling of the water.

By the middle of the afternoon he was ready to set off the powder. Olaf stopped to fill his rank pipe. "Will this put water back in the river?"

"Some," Brad admitted. He stretched muscles unaccustomed to this kind of work. The hard, angry light of remembrance flickered in his gray eyes. "But not fast enough. We owe Quarles something, Olaf. Let's get started giving it to him."

Uncomprehending, but willing, Olaf followed Brad. They took the remaining powder and fuse and on horseback rode above the meadow, dropping down the west side. Brad paused above the point where the water drained into Quarles' reservoir.

There was no sign of anyone. Brad could see some distance through the heat haze dancing down in the valley, but he could make out no movement. Satisfied, he pointed down to the storage lake Quarles had created.

"There's something else that nature didn't do," he told Olaf. "That lucky shale slide of Quarles' just don't look right blocking off all this water. My guess is there'd be a good grass-bottomed draw under there." He paused, and the tight smile settled on his lips again. "I'd even guess it was on my homestead, wouldn't you, Olaf?"

Understanding came to Olaf, and a grin stretched his broad face. "Yah," he agreed. "Too much water."

"Too much of everything for one man," Brad said, and rode ahead down a narrow trail until he came to the base of the shale slide. It towered above him, a great mass of rock and trees that had been swept from a now barren hillside to the east. Nature had provided a narrow bottlenecked draw and a rocky hill ideal for blasting. But she had not provided the providence of a slide to block the draw. Quarles had done that, and Brad felt a thin amusement at reversing the process.

Stationing Olaf on guard, he studied the slide and placed his powder. He decided on two blasts, the first to break the dam, the second to come seconds later and free the rubble that would result. Carefully measuring his fuses, he laid them to a fair distance. Then he drew out a match.

With a troubled glance about him, Brad hesitated. This, he knew, was more than just releasing water the Split S and Jim Parker could use. It was more than just hitting Quarles to draw him into the open. It was more than just vengeance on his own part. He was troubled because he saw the implcations of what might come of this. Quarles had the most men and so the most power. If Brad's gamble failed and the apathy of the other ranchers in the valley was not destroyed, Quarles could gain control with little effort on his part.

Then, Brad reflected, his action would be destroying instead of saving. He would bring war, not the peace he sought.

Momentarily he stayed with the match in his hand, squatted on his bootheels, the decision tugging at his mind. With a sudden, quick motion, he lit the match and touched it to the fuses.

Brad had calculated well. He and Olaf were back on the rimrock above the water when the first blast shook the ground beneath them and a great spume of rock and dust rose in the air. The second blast was an instant later, thundering out before the echoes of the first had got well started.

They sat their horses, looking down and waiting. The dust and the roar went on, seeming to stretch interminably. For a moment, Brad thought he had failed. There was nothing on the surface of the water but ripples caused by raining rock. And then, with a jarring suddenness, he heard the rumbling push as the last of the dam gave and the ever-pressing water sought the level below.

The rumble became a roar as the force of the water worked through the narrow gap the blast had made. Great rocks that had barely stirred beneath the powder began to move, grinding and grumbling, giving way reluctantly. Then, with a sound that shattered the dust-laden air, the last of the barrier gave, and the water gushed out to drop to the bed of the river below.

"Yah!" Olaf cried. "Water back in the river!"

Brad squinted toward the slanting sun. It was almost down behind the western ridges, and he reined the palomino back toward the meadow. Once there he hurriedly set the two charges he had placed that morning.

They were as nothing compared to the great blast down below, but they did what he wanted, settling rock and rubble across the opening and damming up the meadow water until, inevitably, it would flow back into its old channel.

The first darkness was settling in when Brad squatted before their small fire fixing supper. "That water's had about time to reach town," he told Olaf. "See to your guns."

It came sooner than he had expected. The sound of water working its way across the meadow dulled the noise until it was almost on them. The sounds of hoofs clicking on rock came first from the ridge directly behind them, and Brad knew their camp had been sighted.

"Coming," he said briefly to Olaf. He rose from where he sat and threw dirt, piled for the purpose, over the coals of their fire. "Watch west," he warned. "They might snipe from the ridge over there."

"Yah," Olaf agreed softly, from his crouched position behind a stack of supplies.

Brad slipped through the near darkness along the ledge that led to the narrow cut they had brought the supplies through. He was thankful the horses were tethered some distance up, in a grassy clearing, instead of here where they might get hurt. He clambered silently over rock, moving like a shadow behind the barren boulders that marked the cut.

In the last of the light he could make them out dimly, and he counted six picking their way across the jumble of rock from the southeast.

"Far enough," he called out.

The lead man spoke. Brad recognized the voice as Clip's. "Ride out, Jordan," he ordered. "Quarles said to give you a chance to go."

"Even after today?" Brad asked mockingly.

"Yes."

Brad waited a moment. The men had stopped and were watching him. "No," he said finally. "I like it here. I'll stay."

Clip gave an order, unintelligible to Brad, and the men spread, sifting off into the quickening dark. Clip lifted his gun and fired twice into the air. Brad sent a chance shot at the place where the gunflashes had showed, but Clip's answering shot came from some distance to the left.

Very soon Brad realized the significance of the shots. From across the meadow bullets picked their way toward Olaf. Brad could hear them whining off rock, and then he heard the sharp retort from Olaf's gun.

From ahead Clip's men sent a volley at the rock and Brad picked a likely flash to answer. There was a startled curse and he knew he had made his hit. They tried rushing him then, coming in fast, hoping for protection in the darkness. Brad let the carbine drop and used his .44. Behind rock as he was, they could not get to him unless they circled—and it was this he watched for.

He saw a shape loom to the left, sliding up rocks not ten feet away, and his shot brought the man first to his feet and then crashing over backward to tumble limply down.

Clip's sharp order sent another volley at Brad and, laughing softly, he answered rapidly twice. One man shouted something, and Clip's reply rose in a vicious curse.

"Run then, damn you! He ain't but one man."

"The hell he ain't," the voice answered. "That last shot came from the south."

Another man yelled, and now Brad could hear the careful sniping from the south. There was a surge of hoofbeats as men mounted their horses and ran, leaving Clip to curse them, take a last shot, and follow. For an instant he was outlined against the sky and Brad fired. He saw Clip rise in the saddle and then grab as if for the horn. He hung on as the horse charged out of sight over the rough rocks.

Brad waited until the sounds had faded and then he slipped back cautiously to the overhang. The sniping from the far side of the meadow continued; once a bullet struck a case of canned milk, and some trickled sluggishly through the hole in the wooden crate. But now it was growing very dark and with sharp suddenness the gun across the way stopped.

Olaf was not in sight, and Brad was puzzled until he decided he was still south. But it was more than an hour before a wary voice brought Brad alert.

"Here!"

Olaf came slipping in, holding his carbine under his arm. He crouched in the dimness and raked together sticks for a fire. "Coffee," he said.

"And bring their fire on us?"

"Two across the meadow," Olaf said. "No more now."

So that was where he had been. Brad said then, "Make it small."

"Yah," Olaf said, striking a match. The light brought his face into view and Brad noticed that the bitterness that had come to the big sailor so recently was still on his features. From a peaceful man intent on minding his own

business, Olaf had changed to fit the pattern of the country. That was the thing men like Quarles did with their
bullying power and, at the thought, the anger rose hotly
in Brad.

"You got two," Olaf said suddenly. He set the coffeepot over the flames. "And hurt Clip?"

Olaf had been other places besides the far ridge, Brad
realized. "They packed them all off, then?"

"Yah," Olaf said. He pushed the coffeepot impatiently
into the hotter flame.

"Next time Quarles will send a bigger crew," Brad said.

Olaf got up, getting cups and a can of milk. "He'll wait
to hear from them?" When Brad nodded, he smiled a
little, reminiscently. "Won't hear tonight," he added,
putting a stick on the fire.

Brad felt a little sick, dreading this sign of brutality in
a man so naturally gentle. "You got them all, Olaf?"

"One," Olaf said. "Tied Clip and two others in the old
cabin." He pointed toward his homestead. Then he
reached for the pot and poured two cups of coffee.

CHAPTER TWENTY-TWO

A LONG WITH THE OTHERS in the saloon, Arden hurried
out to see the river. He stood on the bank staring dully
down at the rush of water that was churning past. The
meaning of it came to him slowly; it was too sudden, too
far-reaching for him to comprehend it at once.

He heard the talk moving excitedly from man to man
in the crowd. "Quarles get scared?" "Quarles, hell, I
heard a booming up valley today. This was blasted
loose." It was Coe speaking, a cautious, careful man who
was seldom disbelieved.

"Jordan," someone said. "I heard he told Quarles he was homesteading the meadow up there."

They took it up, moving the name of Jordan around until everyone was convinced he was responsible for this water. "About saves the Split S," one man ventured.

"If it ain't too late," came the answer. "And saves Parker, too."

The name of Jim Parker jerked Dave Arden back to reality. The words that had sifted through his mind began to take on meaning, and the understanding of this followed. It was Jordan. He was in full agreement with that.

To draw out Quarles, Arden thought. That would be Jordan's major reason right now. He moved back from the crowd, excited at the ideas beginning to crowd in on him. This was the time to act. Whatever happened now they would blame on Quarles' rage.

He saw Jim Parker break free of the men and go for his horse. It was growing dark, and Arden slipped away and got his own mount and followed. The germ of the plan Keinlan had put in his mind worked itself out as he kept to the river, staying above Parker and out of sight and earshot. This would be on Quarles' head, and then Arden would have more than just the Split S. Between him and Keinlan they would have the valley.

The possibility firing him, he cut downhill toward Parker. As he neared, he could make out the horse and rider, but now it was too dark for recognition. Carefully, Arden worked out his rope and made it ready. He guessed he would reach Parker shortly before he made the turn up to June Grant's.

Parker rode into the softly flung loop of Arden's rope with no warning. He gave a grunt of surprise as he was jerked out of the saddle, and then the wind was gone as he crashed to the hard-packed ground.

Arden pulled his bandanna over his face to guard against all possibility of recognition as he left his horse and finished the roping job. He rounded up Parker's dun pony and lashed the man in the saddle. Parker was nearly out, too groggy to resist.

That done, Arden made a wide swing of town, leading the other horse, and working back until he came to the edge of Parker's spread. He wanted no slip-ups in this. Stopping the horses, he loosened the ropes enough to let Parker slide to the ground.

Deliberately, he drove his boots into the other man's body. In the darkness he could not see well and most of his kicks were aimless. He jerked Parker to his feet and lashed out with his fists.

"We told you to get out," he said in a rough voice. "This time you get."

Parker was sagging at the knees, but he found strength to work one arm free of the rope and drive an ironhard fist at Arden. It connected with Arden's heavy belt buckle, bringing a grunt of pain from both men. Arden dodged the next blow and threw out a foot, tripping Parker. This time he worked the rope on tight and then returned to his beating.

When Parker buckled into unconsciousness, Arden let up, panting from effort. He struck a match and peered down. Parker was not beat too badly, and with cold methodicalness Arden struck him twice more in the face.

Once again he lifted Parker up and roped him to the saddle. He lashed Parker's horse savagely with the end of the reins and the animal leaped forward, taking off at a headlong gallop toward the gap.

Arden stood and listened, breathing heavily, the reins hanging loosely in his hands. It came to him that the horse might run out into the desert and then there would be no one to know Parker had been driven off.

"By God," he whispered angrily, "I'll let them know it!"

He wheeled his horse and hurried up the road to Parker's small spread. There he found coal oil and threw it hastily against the tinder-dry walls of the few outbuildings. He saved the small house, thinking it might come in handy as a line shack when his graze covered the whole west side.

Without hesitating, Arden threw a match at the coal oil, saw it well lit, and headed his horse along the west ridge for the long ride to find Brad Jordan.

Ike Quarles was pacing the floor of his parlor, stopping to curse Jordan and Nick Biddle alternately. Biddle sat on a chair taking Quarles' rage without answer.

"You want to run Split S beef out of Pine Canyon," Quarles said angrily. "That can wait, I tell you. Get Jordan, that's the first thing."

"You can't get the water back," Biddle said.

Quarles swore again. "I can put the dam back once I move Jordan out. Then it's time to worry about Pine Canyon."

"Clip's taking care of Jordan," Biddle answered placidly.

"He's taking a long time doing it," Quarles answered sourly. "I sent him out as soon as it was dark enough. Jordan's too careful to be caught by daylight." He looked at his watch and was amazed at the hours that had gone by. He stopped talking for a time, but when he did so, he could hear the roar of water mocking him from the river gully below, and he began cursing again.

Over the sound of the water and his own heavy breathing, he heard the sound of a running horse. "Clip," Biddle said.

"One horse," Quarles answered. He went carefully to

the door and stepped onto the veranda. He stood there in the darkness, listening. The horse came openly to the front, and a man slid off to the ground. He took two staggering steps forward and pitched on his face.

Quarles hurried out and bent over him. Rising, he bawled for Biddle. Together they got the man into the house. It was Clip, and he had barely enough strength to talk. Quarles poured two shots of whisky down him before Clip managed to get any words out.

"They beat us off from the meadow," he said. "The Swede slipped around behind and got us. Tied Arny and Bart and me in that old shack of his. I got loose."

"Where are the others?" Quarles demanded.

"Dead," Clip said without emotion. "The boys across the ridge come in?"

"Nobody came in."

"The Swede got them, too, then," Clip said. His head dropped. "Arny and Bart'll be along. They're bringing the others."

Quarles stepped away from the couch, his wrath too deep to find relief in swearing. He thought he would burst with it, and it was some time before he could fight himself quiet enough to think clearly.

He stepped to the veranda and stared out at the darkened fields. He could hear the roar of water below, and he turned his eyes bitterly toward town. It was then he saw the distant flame, no bigger than a campfire from where he stood. But he was too old a hand at the ways of this country not to understand. He went inside.

"Looks like Parker's been fired."

"Jordan do that, too?" Biddle asked. There was no intentional humor in him. "Maybe to get you blamed."

"He's been pecking at me like a crazy rooster," Quarles said. He clenched his heavy hands and let them fall open. His deep-set eyes studied Biddle until the other man grew uncomfortable. "That wasn't Jordan," Quarles said thoughtfully. "He wouldn't have had time to get there." He took a short turn about the room and faced Biddle again. "You get rid of Jordan. I'm through nursing him along. There's no law that says a man can't fight back when he's hit."

Biddle said, "Jordan? Me and the crew?"

"You alone. Now!"

Fear was plain in Biddle, but he swallowed it back—his thick hands working together the only sign he failed to hide. "How?" he demanded. He looked meaningly toward the now sleeping Clip.

"How? You made a living tracking Indians once, didn't you? You ought to know how."

"Jordan ain't no Indian. I'd rather go after a dozen Indians."

Quarles curbed his anger with an effort. "I want Jordan and that Swede out of the way. Tonight. Then fix it so they can't be found until we want them found. After that, you take care of Arden. I want him near Jordan. I want it done to look like they got each other."

Biddle nodded and got up reluctantly. He saw to his gun and worked his hat over his head. "Be quiet about it," Quarles warned. "Jordan's no fool."

"So I know," Biddle said.

He took it slowly, fearing the idea of riding alone on Brad Jordan. The nearer he got to the foot of the meadow the colder his sweat ran. He lingered, seeking some excuse that Quarles would accept. But he realized that Quarles would be satisfied only with the job done. Slowly, he pushed his horse up into the hils. If he wanted his share of the valley, he would have to do his share of the work.

It seldom occurred to Biddle that Quarles sent him on most of the dangerous jobs. Quarles did the planning—

something Biddle knew he had little talent for. He accepted the situation. But now, remembering his last brush with Jordan, and remembering what had happened to Clip, he had no liking at all for the work. What if Jordan had moved out of the meadow and was watching the trail? What if he, Biddle, didn't hit square the first shot? What then?

He stopped again, still some distance below the mouth of the meadow. He had chosen to go this way hoping he could find a route that would make less noise. He figured they would have a watch from the back, and he had no desire to get into what Clip had. If he could come up from the front he might have a chance.

He was ready to start again when he heard the sounds of hoofbeats hurrying up from below. He sucked in his breath, and in a panic rushed his horse off the trail into a nest of scrub fir. Had Jordan trailed him, first hiding below to watch?

His hand trembled as he pulled out his gun, and he put the other hand on the horse's neck to quiet it. The rider below was coming closer fast, hitting a good clip.

Biddle tried to see out of his screen of trees, but they gave him no sight of the trail at all. He could do nothing but wait and listen, trying to judge when the horse reached him.

The rider was almost before him when Biddle took a final breath and plunged into the open. One hand held his gun and the other a match. He said, "Hold it up," and struck the match.

He saw Arden's twisted face and saw Arden go for his gun. He cried, "Biddle here!"

Arden's face relaxed, and Biddle let the match drop to the dirt, where it went out. He remembered Quarles' telling him that Arden was against him and so, though he made a pretense of holstering his gun, he kept it lying in shadow along his leg.

"Jordan's in the meadow," Biddle said. He was thinking that this would please Quarles—his getting both Arden and Jordan at the same time.

Arden's mind had caught at this new development and was working it over. He had thought about Biddle, but during the last few hours it had gone from his mind. Now the idea he had once pondered returned, and he took it back quickly. He had only to get Biddle to Jordan's camp, shoot him, drawing Jordan out by the noise, and then pick Jordan off. It would leave the blame on Biddle and, therefore, on Quarles. It was that simple.

Now he loosened his gun and dropped his horse back to be alongside Biddle. He was pleased at this night's work and felt the need for boasting. Who better to listen than one of the men who had planned to rob him of his share in the valley?

He kept the gun across his lap, but away from Biddle so it could not be seen. His voice was amused as he spoke. "I burned Parker out tonight. Beat and ran him out, too."

Biddle's slow wits were quick enough to warn him to caution. "Why?"

Arden laughed a little. "Keinlan and me figured it out. He'll take the town and I'll take the valley. You and Quarles won't be here, Nick."

Biddle could feel the cold breath of hell on his neck. "Why?" he asked again.

"They'll run Quarles out for burning Parker," Arden said. "And you're going to bait a trap for Jordan." His laugh came a second time, a little unsteady. "Don't try anything. I got my gun."

He was still trying to say it, still laughing nervously when Biddle's gun lifted from the shadow of his leg and fired. The second shot hit Arden before he could feel the blow of the first.

Biddle pulled his horse back and watch Arden pitch out of the saddle and land soggily on the trail. It came to him that he had shot too soon. It wasn't far to the meadow, and Jordan might have heard the gun. The idea worked in him like warm yeast, and in a sudden panic he swung down trail and raced wildly for the valley.

CHAPTER TWENTY-THREE

BIDDLE rode into Quarles' yard, still going as if pursued by devils. He left the saddle, hardly seeing the strange horse tethered close by, and bulled his way into the house. Panting, he leaned against the wall.

Keinlan was sitting relaxed in a chair. He looked around, saw Biddle, and continued with what he was saying. Quarles started to interrupt, then turned his back on Biddle.

"They think you did it," Keinlan was saying. "They think you rode on Parker. More'n one's getting scared you're going after them and the town because the water got loose. They're talking about a posse."

"Posse be damned!" Quarles roared.

He fought to choke back his rage. Taking a cigar from his case, he took out a match. But he kept the cigar unlighted in his fingers. "I'll ride in and talk to them," he said. "Hell, I burned nobody. That ain't my way."

"You think they'll listen?" Keinlan asked softly. "You ever see a burning crew, Quarles? It's like a lynching mob. They go crazy. You can't talk to crazy men." Quarles started for the door, and Keinlan added, "What are you going to do?"

Quarles wheeled about, flinging the still unlighted match savagely to the floor. "Get my crew. No one's going to burn me out!"

Biddle broke in. "Ike, I got Arden."

"Shut up. You didn't get Jordan. I can see that."

Keinlan rose, smiling his peculiar smile. "Play it the way you want," he said. "I'll go back to work."

He had passed Quarles and was nearly to the door, when Quarles said, "What other way is there? What would you do?"

"I wouldn't pull into my hole," Keinlan said. This was the time he had been waiting for, and he spoke cautiously, making sure there would be no mistakes. "What if you do beat them off? You're done here. You make a stand now and you'll crawl forever after."

It was a long speech for him, and he paused to let it take effect. "If it was me," he said, "I'd keep prodding. They think you started it. All right, finish it." His voice rose. "Hit them hard enough and they'll stop being crazy. They were afraid before. Make them afraid again. Keep them that way. Ride down before they can ride on you!"

Quarles' hoarse breathing was the only sound for a long moment. "I'll wait no more," he said softly. "Go hole up in your saloon so you don't get shot." His laughter was without amusement.

Keinlan walked silently out of the house and got to his horse. He was in the saddle when he heard Biddle bawl, "Ike, listen——"

"Shut up. We got got things to do."

Biddle waited no longer. He jerked his gun free. stepped to the veranda and fired at Keinlan. Keinlan felt the slug tear into him, throwing him forward across the saddle horn. Instinctively, he kicked at his horse and raced off as two more bullets spatted angrily. He felt one nick the cantle, and the other found its mark on him. He rolled in the saddle but kept his seat, and soon he was on the road and out of range.

"You crazy fool," Quarles shouted at Biddle.

Resentfully, Biddle told him what Arden had said. Quarles was silenced, his eyes narrowing, seeking a meaning to this. He said, finally, "He stirred the town and then he stirs me. I was to ride into a trap. Go after him."

"He won't get far," Biddle said. "I hit him too square."

Quarles turned as if this was enough to make him forget Keinlan. "They expect us to ride. We'll ride," he said grimly. "Go get your crew ready. We'll meet at your place. We'll hit the Split S and then town. They want burning—we'll give them burning."

Keinlan kept hitting feebly at the horse, forcing it to greater speed. Though the jolting was almost beyond what he could bear, he knew there was just so much life in him, and he wanted to save it until he reached town.

He was not bitter. He had realized the chance he took, and it was a matter of some surprise to him that this had not been done before.

He saw the town ahead and knew he could make it. The horse was stumbling from weariness, lathered heavily, but it kept going until Keinlan managed to pull up before the sheriff's office. He cried out McFee's name, and then he could hold on no longer He went out of the saddle and sprawled in the dust of the street.

McFee and Faith helped him into the jail office. He was bleeding freely, and the pain that twisted his long, odd face was etched deeply. He managed to say, "Quarles is riding."

Faith stood back and, without fastidiousness, wiped his blood from her hands. "On June?" she asked.

"Split S is on his way to town," Keinlan said. "Warn her."

Faith scooped a rifle from the rack behind the sheriff's desk and hurried out. "Tell the others," she called back to her uncle.

"Wait," Keinlan said to McFee. "I got something to say."

McFee tried to get him to a chair, but Keinlan folded to the floor. "Leave me be," he said painfully. "Not much time." He began to talk slowly, with a great deal of effort. He told about his plans and about Arden. He told McFee Arden's scheme to cross Quarles. He said that Biddle had got Arden. When he had finished, he fumbled uncertainly for a cigar.

McFee got it for him and struck a match. "I'm going after the Doc," he said.

"Not time enough," Keinlan answered.

McFee watched the cigar smoke slide in slowly and come out in a painful cloud. Keinlan was even smiling a little. McFee said, "What did you want? Wasn't a good living enough?"

"A living?" Keinlan coughed, and the effort brought fresh sweat to his face. "No, I wanted more. A man always does. What's a living?" He spoke haltingly. "But I didn't want Quarles sharing it. His greed is too big. Never give anything to Quarles' kind. I wanted more—but he wanted it all."

He coughed again, and his voice came slower, weaker. "Remember that, never give anything to his kind."

"I'll remember," McFee said grimly.

"If you live long enough," Keinlan answered. The cigar fell from his fingers and hissed out in a pool of blood seeping from under him. "Arden didn't get what he wanted any more than I did," he added.

"I'll find the Doc," McFee said again. But when he looked at Keinlan he could see it would be no use. Putting the dead man's hat over his face, the sheriff hurried out.

Brad heard the two shots and came alert. He caught the sound of a horse running rapidly, and the fact that it was fading puzzled him. By the stars he judged that it was close to midnight, and he suspected it was about time for another attack by Double Q.

When there were no further sounds, he slipped out of the overhang with Olaf and got their horses. They worked carefully around the meadow until they were on the trail. From a small bench that overlooked the valley the last of Parker's fire caught Brad's eye.

"Burning," he said. His voice was low and hard.

"Split S?" Olaf asked.

"South of town. I'd say Parker." He paused. "It will be Split S next, if that's so."

They went on down the trail, and before long Brad discovered the reason for the shots. He left the saddle at the sight of the dark mound lying in his path. He lit a match and bent, studying Arden in silence.

Olaf said in a puzzled voice, "Here's a horse." And drew a saddle animal from where it had been rein-caught in a patch of buckbrush.

"Arden's," Brad said. "Someone shot him twice and ran."

Olaf led the horse up silently. Together, they got Arden's body into the saddle and rode on down the trail. At the bottom, Brad hurried toward town.

He looked toward the Split S, but could see only the pinpoints of light that showed June Grant was there and awake. He thought of turning off to see her when a fast-moving horse pulled him up by the turn. It came steadily on, and he held his gun in readiness, his eyes bleak and waiting.

By now his eyes were accustomed to the darkness, and

he could see that the rider was a woman. Her startled gasp echoed in his ears as she realized someone blocked her way.

"Brad Jordan," he identified himself. "Who is it?"

Her voice sounded relieved. "Faith McFee."

"What was the burning?"

"Jim Parker," she answered. "Just the outbuildings. He can't be found."

"Quarles rode him out. Just as he tried to do us," Brad said.

"That's what we think." She told him about Keinlan. "Quarles will hit June. I've come to warn her." She rode closer to Brad and saw the third horse. "Someone else?" she asked bitterly.

Brad could only say, "Arden."

"Dave? Is—is he——?" She stopped.

"Yes," he said flatly.

She said abruptly, bitterly, "Because you thought he was turning on June, you killed——"

Brad interrupted harshly, "No!" He left it there a moment in silence. "I found him this way," he said finally.

He wished that she would believe him and then turn her mind back to the business at hand. It would be better. But her silence told him that his words had meant nothing.

"After the way you acted," she began.

His voice was rough, short. "I promised the sheriff I'd tend to June Grant's business. I've done that, and I'll keep on doing that. Killing Arden wasn't part of the agreement, so I didn't do it."

His sarcasm seemed to have missed her. She said, "But you still think that Dave was in with Quarles?"

He said levelly, "Yes. But there's no time for that now. I'll ride to Split S. You get back to town and warn them about Quarles."

"They're warned," she said. There was a pause. Then her voice came cold and dead, "What about Dave?"

"I hadn't thought," Brad admitted.

She untied the reins from Brad's saddle and fastened them to her own. "I'll take him in," she said, and rode away.

Brad started up the road to the Split S. By her tone of voice he could tell that she still refused to believe him.

As he rode along he turned it over in his mind. Whatever interest he might have had in Faith McFee had best be killed now, he thought grimly. What woman would think about a man she believed had shot her future husband?

It surprised him to find that he thought of her in that way. Otherwise, he knew, he would not have been so affected by her praise or scorn for him, so upset by her doubts. The thought disturbed him.

But he thrust it aside. There were other things to do. The death of Arden was just one link in this chain that seemed ready to come to an end. His dream of land and peace still lay ahead, and it was Quarles who lay between it and himself now.

He said to Olaf, "Let's hurry. We've got business to attend to."

CHAPTER TWENTY-FOUR

THERE WAS A LIGHT in the bunkhouse and one in the parlor at the Split S. Brad rode into the lamplight coming from the open bunkhouse door and swung to the ground. Nate Krouse came out, looking curious, and Brad thought how easy it would be for someone to take this place.

"Jordan," Brad told him. He tossed his reins to Olaf and strode around to the front of the house. He could hear Krouse talking to Olaf, but the words were too low for him to catch.

June Grant let him in. He saw that the frown of worry had deepened in her forehead until an almost permanent groove had been cut there.

"I thought it might be Jim," she said. "He was supposed to come." She stepped aside, letting Brad by. "I have you to thank for the water?"

"No thanks needed," he said. "It brought Quarles out of his hole." He disliked telling her this, feeling that a good deal of the blame was on his head. But there was no other way.

"Parker's outbuildings were burned. In town they think he was run out."

She was very quiet, her hands hanging limply at her sides, her face slightly tilted so that the lamplight etched her gentle profile. "I knew the fire was Jim's. But I—I kept hoping."

Brad went on ruthlessly, "And Quarles is riding." He told her what Faith had said. "He may come here first."

June turned, starting for the door. "I'll tell the men," she said. "Dave isn't here or he might——"

"Arden is dead," Brad said. "I found him on the trail up to the meadow."

Her face twisted back over her shoulder, and for a moment her eyes tugged at his and then dropped away. "You—no, you didn't."

"Faith won't believe that," he told her.

"She was shocked," June Grant said, and went out through the kitchen. Brad followed her and stepped to the yard just as she was calling the men from the bunkhouse.

"Quarles is riding on the town," June said without pre-amble. "He may hit here first. He burned Jim out to-night."

"Town?" Andy Toll echoed. His empty expression became startled and then worried. "Where can we go if he hits town?"

"You can stay here," Brad said.

"Thirty men if he gets Sawhorse in, too," Nate Krouse said. He spat at the ground and ducked his head, not looking at anyone.

"Or you can ride over the mountains and try to find another home," Brad added.

"There ain't no place," Andy Toll said plaintively. He looked around, as if realizing a threat to his security for the first time. "What's he want to bother us for?"

Nat Krouse lifted his head suddenly and walked into the bunkhouse. He came out strapping on a gun belt and awkwardly holding a carbine under one arm. There was a faint smile hovering on his lips as he looked past June Grant at Brad.

"I'm too old to find another home," he said.

Jake Bannon had been silent, rocking back and forth on his toes, looking first at one thing and then at another. Now he said something inaudible and ducked into the bunkhouse. He came out, as Krouse had, with his guns.

"You'd better ride, Andy," June Grant said. But there was a gladness in her voice directed at the other two men.

"Take Miss June into town and go on," Brad said.

She spun around. "I'm not going to town! This is my home. I'll be the last to leave it."

"She can shoot, too," Krouse remarked, as she started briskly toward the house. He spat a second time. "Tuck up your skirts and start riding, Andy."

Andy Toll's face worked. "What's he want to do this for?" he demanded. There was no answer from anyone.

He made an empty sound and walked slowly into the bunkhouse. Brad could see him through the door, pawing over his war bag. He came out and got two horses from the corral, saddling one and putting his pack on the other. He mounted.

June Grant came from the house and handed him some money. "Your wages," she said. "Thanks, Andy, you've been a good hand."

He took the money. "You didn't hire me for fighting," he blurted, and kicked at the horse he rode.

They watched him go out of the light into shadow, and finally there was only the sound of hoofs on the dry roadway. The last sound was the faint rumble of planks as he crossed the bridge.

"If they come, it'll be soon," Brad said. "Let's get ready."

"You're helping?" June asked.

Brad looked at her. "Some people will think I caused it," he said. "I'm helping."

They were watching him, and he realized then it was not for censure but for leadership. He said, "Let's get the horses where they'll be safe but handy. That's the first thing."

They did so, choosing a place near the front of the house out of possible lines of fire, and in shadow. Each of the men made a pack and, with the greatest reluctance, June Grant did the same thing.

Suddenly there was no more time. Brad heard it first—a low distant rumbling like far thunder. There was no doubt of it as the noise increased.

"They're riding," he said.

Krouse cocked his head. "Coming here, too. They're in Biddle's upper pasture now."

Brad directed them quickly, putting Bannon and Krouse in the big barn and June in the upper part of the house. He stationed Olaf in the shadow of a great cotton-wood, where he would have a full sweep of the yard. The bunkhouse light went out, and those in the house as well.

From the barn loft, Nate Krouse said, "I'm kinda glad it's come. It had to sooner or later."

"Shoot only when there's something to hit," Brad warned, and rode his palomino back into shadow near the front of the house.

The silence came down heavily now, broken only by the steady thundering sound. Then that splintered, and Brad could catch the individual beat of horses moving fast over hard-packed earth. They were less than five minutes away, on Split S range, and riding downhill.

Krouse called, "Both crews coming."

Brad drew his carbine and moved around to the north side of the house, stationing himself there against a pro-tective corner of the kitchen wing. He judged that they would ride in between the two barns—the big one where Krouse and Bannon were, and the older, smaller one that was empty except for some cast-off saddle gear.

When they came it was in a long line, two and three abreast. The darkness obviously confused them, for they drew up with ten men in the yard and the others halting behind.

"Ride back," Brad called to them. "There's nothing here."

"Jordan!" It was Quarles' voice, and in the one word Brad could sense his surging, uncontrolled anger. Quarles had lost his iron grip on himself, Brad realized, and he was turning his unthinking rage on everything in his path, whereas he had turned it only on Parker before.

"Hit them!" Quarles shouted.

"That's warning enough," Brad said, and fired. On the echo of his shot four others came, almost simultaneously. There was a yelling and a whinny as a horse went down.

One man swore in pain and another in anger. The horses in the yard began to mill as the men behind couldn't get out of the way fast enough. Brad fired again. And from Olaf's position another shot came.

Those in the yard were shooting now, but ineffectually against the dark. From the house and the barn loft, June and her men picked their targets carefully.

Quarles roared an order and the remaining men swung and formed, racing out of range behind the big barn. Shots were coming from the far edge of the yard; Brad heard one strike against the house. The men out there were shooting with rifles now.

Four men lay in the yard, one crawling through the dirt, the others still. A riderless horse was tugging to free his reins from a dead man's grip, and another horse was down, kicking and making a screaming sound. A bullet from the attic stilled it.

The silence came and was broken again. "They're circling," Krouse called out. His gun made a spatting sound. "Torch," he said.

His gun cracked again. Brad withdrew from his position and rode away from the house southward until he had a view of the area behind the barns. A man with a torch was riding in a weaving pattern, trying to work his fire up against whatever he could reach. He angled out of range of the men in the barn and was almost to the building when Brad's careful shot drove him out of the saddle. He threw the torch as he fell, and it landed in dry grass that had been let grow raggedly behind the barn.

Brad stayed where he was, watching the fire grow, his eyes bleak with the realization of helplessness. Then the flames leaped high enough for him to be a target, and three guns crashed, driving him back. He wheeled into the yard and looked briefly down at the men on the ground. He knew none of them.

Brad worked his way back to the shadow of the house. He could hear the gentle crackle of flames even from where he sat his horse, and the smell of smoke was strong on the southwest wind. Without warning, the crackle grew to a roar and a spurt of flame shot into the air.

"Barn's caught," Jake Bannon cried in panic. And Brad saw him poised at the edge of the haymow. He stood an instant and then jumped, hit the ground ten feet below, staggered forward and ran for the horses.

"Not this barn," Krouse shouted uselessly after him.

Someone shot from between the barns, and Bannon made a loop in the air and landed belly down in the dust. Brad fired at the man who had slipped quietly up. He got an answering shot and returned it, and the man came into the open holding his stomach and vomiting. Brad saw Nate Krouse poised above, and then Nate's bullet drilled the man in the head, dropping him.

The old barn was burning faster now, pushed by the breeze and its own ancient dryness. Brad called, "Come down," to Krouse, who disappeared from the haymow. In a moment he reached the yard, hesitated, and raced for the protection of the bunkhouse. A gun began to spit, spurting dust around his feet, but he danced his way into darkness, and the gun ceased.

Shortly he came alongside Brad, his voice coming harshly through his winded breathing. "That barn'll light the whole place up in a minute."

"Gives us something to aim by," Brad answered.

"All right," Krouse said, and retreated.

Shots began to come from behind now, and Brad realized they were circled. He heard Olaf's answer, and then Nate Krouse shooting from near the bunkhouse. There was the sound of an attic window going up and June Grant's carbine was loud.

Brad pushed his carbine into the boot and drew his .44. Turning the palomino, he worked outward in darkness. He saw a man sliding Indian-fashion through the grass. Brad shot, and the man stopped, his gun in one outstretched hand.

Brad worked the edges, finding some advantage in this sniping, but knowing it could not go on. The barn was burning harder and brighter, throwing its light farther with each minute. There was an explosion of tinder-dry wood, and before long the bunkhouse roof caught and it, too, began to roar.

Time seemed to stand still as Quarles' men worked in and out, also keeping to shadow, and aiming for the house. There were only sporadic shots now from both sides. Brad was near the veranda when he caught the sound of rushing hoofs, and turned to see a small group spearheading for the edge of the yard. He shouted, "Olaf!" and fired into the group. Olaf's carbine took up the fight, and the men broke, splitting and fading to the sides. Olaf rode from his protection, still firing, and Brad rode off at an angle, reaching the two men who had broken to the north. He knocked one man sidewise in the saddle, and felt the sharp stabbing pain of lead burning his arm before both men dipped down out of sight.

A great tongue of flame leaped high as a section of barn roof crashed in throwing heat and sparks far around it. Brad wheeled his horse to get back into shadow, and came against another rider. He swung his gun about when he recognized Faith McFee. Her horse was heavily lathered and, even in the dimness, Brad could see the signs of strain and weariness on her face.

He pulled her into deeper shadow. "What are you doing here?"

"What is there for me in town?" she asked. He did not

answer. And she went on, "Molly Teehan brought Jim Parker in to the Doc. He was run out as you were." There was a blank emptiness in her voice. "Keinlan told my uncle that it was Dave who did it, not Quarles."

Brad rocked in the saddle. "It's Quarles doing this," he said. "Are we getting help?"

Her voice was bitter. "When I left Molly Teehan had only two men rounded up. The rest were running for holes."

Brad rode away from the house a short way and called softly to June Grant. In a moment she came down, slipping through shadow to him. He told her what Faith had reported.

"Ride out of here. Tell Molly Teehan to take Jim Parker back to the gap where he'll be safe. He'll have a chance there."

"And you?"

"I'll work the edges for a while," Brad said. "Maybe we can hold them here until the town's ready. If it ever is."

"I'm staying," she said flatly.

Brad worked shells into his gun. The shots were scattered now. "You can rebuild a home. You can't rebuild a man. You go see to Parker."

Faith McFee rode up. "They're not sending help," she said to June.

June Grant moved away beside Faith's horse, her straight back bowed, her head down. Brad pushed the palomino around to the far side of the house where no firelight yet reached and kept watch again.

After a while Faith rode up to him. "She's below the bridge," she said.

"You should have gone. There's nothing for you here."

"Someone to ride with," she said. He could see her face only briefly, but her expression was set.

"The man who shot Arden," he told her.

"No," she answered. "I heard the truth. It was Nick Biddle. Before I got to town I knew I was wrong." There was no apology in her voice.

Brad looked away. He was seeing her now as he had visualized all women during his drifting life. Quiet and grave and steady—someone to stand by a man.

"This is foolishness," he said sharply. "Ride while you can."

A splatter of shots cut off her reply. From over where Olaf would be, a drumming of gunfire rose. And two quick bursts came from the south where Krouse had ridden.

Brad felt lead whip at his hatbrim and the flash was almost upon him. He said savagely, "Ride back," to Faith, and answered the shot.

Another followed it, and then a fulsillade from three different places. Quarles, in his fury, was not leaving until he had burned Split S to the ground. Under cover of heavy firing, he would drive his men at the house. This much Brad knew, and he realized there were too many to handle angling toward him.

"Come back," Faith cried at him. Her gun beat nearby, holding them off.

He rode back, bitter at being driven away, but realizing the futility of it. They kept going back, firing as a swarm of men worked forward, coming out of the dark on two sides, coming in on them with a squeezing pincer movement.

Brad spoke to Faith and saw her reach Olaf's side, and then he broke through a patch of glaring light for cover. A gun's roar rose in the smoky air, and the bullet was like a sledge across his arm, half knocking him from the saddle. The other wound had been only a burn; this felt as if it had taken his arm away at the shoulder. He lay flat and urged his horse on.

And out of the crackle of flames and the sharpness of gunfire rose Quarles' hoarse voice. "There's Jordan. Get that drifter."

Brad reached the shadow, his arm hanging limp. He heard Faith's quick, indrawn breath. Olaf was crouching over his horse, the carbine still barking its steady sounds. From the left, Nate Krouse came weaving in. He was almost to shadow when a bullet jerked a leg from under him, and he sprawled forward, sliding the rest of the way.

Olaf went off his horse and lifted the smaller man, flinging him behind the saddle. Faith said, "They're circling again, Brad. Come on."

He fired a last shot and holstered his gun so he could use his right hand for the reins. There was a moment of suspension while Nate Krouse was transferred to his own horse, and then they raced for the road as a cross-fire cut savagely at them.

Brad rode low, angrily, knowing that Quarles had won this hand. They got over the rise and down almost to the bridge when the sound of men coming behind them rose over the roar of the fire. Brad looked back, and by the light of the burning buildings he made out the entire crew streaming over the rise. He could see the hugeness of Quarles in the lead.

"Hurry!" Faith pleaded from beside him. "He's left the house alone. It's you he wants. You first, and then everything else."

CHAPTER TWENTY-FIVE

Within sight of the town limits Olaf's horse failed. The bay had already put forth more effort than Brad had believed possible, and now he was done. He stopped, his head hanging and his muscles quivering.

Behind and on the slopes above, the Sawhorse and Double Q riders were closing in swiftly. Brad and Olaf together quickly unsaddled the bay and turned him loose. Then Olaf put Faith on the palomino with Brad and squeezed himself into her smaller saddle. They hurried on.

But the delay had narrowed the already dangerous margin, and three hard rifleshots slapped by them as they reached the restaurant.

Angus McFee appeared in the jailhouse door. "In here," he said briefly.

Faith stumbled wearily as Brad helped her to the ground. He threw his good arm around her and supported her inside. Olaf came after them, carrying Nate Krouse as if he were of no weight. McFee kicked shut the door, and with a rifle butt hammered out the glass of a front window.

He was talking, harsh and angry. "June rode back. The Doc sent Parker to the gap with Tim. Molly and June wouldn't go."

The crew, spearheaded by Quarles, burst into town as if they were free to take it over. There was a minute of heavy silence. And then from all sides—the saloons, the livery, and even the general store—came a burst of withering fire. The men shouted in sudden terror and, without trying to return the fire, broke for the dark safety of the lanes between buildings.

"Looks to me like June got more results than just

getting Parker out of town," Brad observed. He stood at the window across the door from the sheriff.

McFee swore dully. "We learned," he said. "Took a lot, but we learned. Even Coe and the east-siders are up on the roof of Doc's and Keinlan's."

He levered a cartridge into his rifle. "Shooting in my town," he said angrily, as another lone gunshot went off from the west.

When he looked around his lined, wizened face was set as Brad had never seen it. "Damn them all," he said, and jerked open the door.

Brad started forward and then stopped, returning to the window. McFee walked to the street and turned, going down the middle, the rifle cradled in his arm. His voice rose in the dead silence. He walked past the three men who had died in the last volley and kept on going.

"Get out of town with your guns!" he shouted. "Take your wars out of here. All of you."

Brad said, "Good God, he'll get——"

He stopped as a heavy figure came on horseback from the lane between the hotel and Keinlan's saloon. It was Quarles, and he sat with his hands spread from his sides.

"I'll tend to your town later," he told McFee. "I want Jordan."

"There'll be no more shooting here," McFee said angrily.

"I want Jordan."

Brad stepped to the door and through it to the steps of the jail. "Here, Quarles." He glanced back at Faith McFee and saw that she had taken his place at the window. He said sharply, "Leave him alone." And her gun lowered.

"You can't——" she began.

"His men quit him," Brad said quietly. "Otherwise,

he'd be trying his power still. Men like that always quit when they face matching odds. The valley should have learned that sooner." He smiled thinly at her and walked down the steps.

Quarles was still motionless, his head swiveling between Brad and McFee's gun. Brad pulled himself into the saddle, his left hand hanging limply in plain sight.

There was a shot that cut air above his horse's neck, and Nick Biddle rode into view, working to get another. The sheriff's gun swiveled around and cracked, and Biddle rose in the stirrups, settled back and dropped limply. His horse neighed and spurted forward, dragging Biddle by one foot down the road and out of sight.

Still Quarles did not move. Brad said, "I'll meet you at the edge of town," and rode on. When he glanced back, Ike Quarles had disappeared from sight, and the sheriff was walking the street still crying his order.

Brad heard a single rider going parallel to him. The darkness was between them—the few lights of the town and the last flames of the Split S being nothing against it. At the town limits sign Brad reined in his horse, and with his one good hand worked at rolling a cigarette.

He had it made and between his lips when the soft steps of Quarles' horse moved nearer. Brad dropped the match he held unlighted and put his hand on his gun.

"You're through, Quarles," he said. "You and Biddle."

The shot came from not twenty feet away, and the burst of gun flame was like Quarles' rage—hot and quick and wild. The bullet went wide in the darkness. Brad drew his own gun carefully. A second shot was at closer range. Now Brad judged the gun flash and fired.

Quarles' cry and his third shot blended as one sound. Brad felt the heavy blow of the bullet kick his leg from the stirrup. He fired again, riding in at Quarles' dark bulk.

He was ready to shoot again, but there was no need.
Quarles was out of the saddle, crawling on the ground,
swearing. He came to his knees as Brad reached him.
Not a foot away lay the gun he had dropped when he
was hit.

"Pick it up," Brad said.

Quarles put his hand on the gun and lifted it. Brad
deliberately shot him between the eyes, threw his weight
to the side, and so guided the palomino back toward
town. He had not got halfway when the pain in his arm
and that in his leg rushed up together and came down
like a club across his skull. He fell forward reaching for
the saddle horn.

He felt the coldness of water on his body and opened
his eyes to see Doc Stebbins staring down at him. He
lifted his head enough to see that Faith was washing
his wounds with a blood-soaked cloth. His levis had been
cut back to the knee, and the sleeve of his shirt was off.
His head dropped back.

"Quarles is out there," he told them.

"The Swede brought him in," the Doc said.

"His crew," Faith told Brad, "rode on like you said."

Doc Stebbins gently pushed Faith aside and began
bandaging. Brad worked tobacco from his pocket, and
with his right hand tried to make a cigarette. Faith took
it and rolled it for him. He let her put it between his
lips and strike a match. He took a deep lungful of smoke,
and then murmured his thanks.

"Maybe you'll have peace for a while now," he said
thoughtfully. "Just watch who you let on the Double Q
and Sawhorse."

From a corner where Brad had not seen him, McFee
said, "I'm having them put up for public sale."

Brad's head turned. "They're not in your town," he said.

McFee stood straighter than Brad had ever seen him, and there was a young look to his weathered face. "I'm the law in the valley," he said. "I've appointed myself so."

"In that case," Brad said, with a faint flash of his old humor, "a man will have to ride clear through the gap to shoot his gun." He closed his eyes.

When he opened them again, he saw that he was alone with Faith McFee. She sat on the sofa beside him and there was a gentleness in her face.

"You're going again?" she asked. "I could see you thinking of it."

"For a time," he admitted. "I thought of riding to the county seat to borrow money. I'd like to buy the Double Q. With Olaf to raise the hay, we could do well."

"There's money here for lending," she said. She leaned closer to him, and a little color stained her cheeks. "I'd like to be partners in a ranch, myself."

Brad took the cold stub of the cigarette from his lips and let it drop to the floor. A sudden light danced up through the pain shadowing his gray eyes.

"You wouldn't want to seal that contract?" he asked.

When she lifted her lips from his, she said gently, "You aren't brutal all the time, are you?"

He was glad to see that there was laughter in her, too. His good arm raised and caught her.

"Just part of the time," he answered, and drew her mouth down hard.

Louis Trimble was born in Seattle, Washington, and during most of his professional career taught in the University of Washington system of higher education. 'I began writing Western fiction,' he later observed, 'because of my interest in the history and physical character of the western United States and because the Western was (and is) a genre in which a writer could move with a great deal of freedom.' His first Western novel under the Louis Trimble byline was *Valley of Violence* (1948). In this and his subsequent Western novels he seems to have been most influenced by Ernest Haycox, another author who lived in the Pacific Northwest. He also used the *nom de plume* **Stuart Brock** under which he wrote five exceptional Westerns, all published by Avalon Books in the 1950s. The point of focus in his Western fiction, whether he is writing as Louis Trimble or Stuart Brock, constantly shifts among various viewpoints and women are often major characters. *Railtown Sheriff* (1949) was Trimble's first Western novel as Stuart Brock and it was under this byline that some of his most exceptional work appeared, most notably *Action at Boundary Peak* and *Whispering Canyon*, both in 1955, and *Forbidden Range* in 1956. These novels have strong characters, complex and realistic situations truly reflecting American life on the frontier, and often there is a mystery element that heightens a reader's interest. The terrain of the physical settings in these stories is vividly evoked and is an essential ingredient in the narrative. Following his retirement from academic work, Trimble made his retirement home in Devon, England.